IT'S A BIT MORE COMPLICATED THAN THAT

IT'S A BIT MORE COMPLICATED THAN THAT

HANNAH MARSHALL

ALLEN&UNWIN
AUCKLAND • SYDNEY • MELBOURNE • LONDON

First published in 2025

Allen & Unwin Aotearoa New Zealand
Level 2, 10 College Hill, Freemans Bay
Auckland 1011, New Zealand
+64 (9) 377 3800
auckland@allenandunwin.com
www.allenandunwin.co.nz

83 Alexander Street
Crows Nest NSW 2065, Australia
+61 (2) 8425 0100

EU Authorised Representative: Easy Access System Europe,
Mustamäe tee 50, 10621 Tallinn, Estonia, gpsr.requests@easproject.com

A catalogue record for this book is available from
the National Library of New Zealand.

ISBN 978 1 991006 94 3

Cover design by Christa Moffitt, Christabella Designs
Text design by Kate Barraclough
Printed and bound in Australia by the Opus Group

1 3 5 7 9 10 8 6 4 2

FSC www.fsc.org MIX Paper | Supporting responsible forestry FSC® C001695

For my friends

PROLOGUE
ZELLE

Cold pavement.

Hot cheek.

Need air.

Need water.

I open my eyes and the light is too much. Animal noises in my throat. Body on fire. Limbs twitching. Bad smell beneath me. A hand on my back — Luka?

Try to speak. No words. No air.

Standing on the edge of an infinitude. I let it swallow me whole.

It burns.

It burns.

It burns.

When I wake up the world rushes in. The fire in my body has dulled to a low flicker, the final embers from a bonfire. But, God, I feel hollow. I'm a shell of a girl. My head spins and my vision's glittery. I realise I must still be slightly drunk.

'Welcome back, Giselle,' a voice says, soft and slightly nasally. Scottish, maybe. Not a voice I know. 'My name's Dr Burns. You're in Wellington Hospital.'

I sit up a little, staring at the IV snaking out of my arm. A mid-thirties woman with slick black hair and thick winged eyeliner is standing at the edge of my bed. I run a shaking hand under my eyes. Silver eyeshadow and smears of mascara stain my fingers.

'Water?' I croak, and Dr Burns reaches over to a glass jug on a small white table. She fills a plastic cup with water, and I down it like it's liquid gold. It's frigid, clinking with ice, exactly what I need right now. I hold my cup out for a refill.

Dr Burns obliges. 'Do you remember what happened tonight, Giselle?' she says, while I scull the second cup. Cold water to soothe hot flames.

A few hours too late for that, I think.

'Zelle,' I say. 'Everyone calls me Zelle.'

'Do you remember what happened, Zelle?'

The night is fractured into shards of memory, pockets of sense. We started with margaritas and tequila shots at Tabitha's before hitting up town. A round of Tennessee Fire at the bar, maybe two. Dancing. Back to the bar for more shots. A Macca's stop at some point, though I didn't want to eat. Staggering out for fresh air onto Courtenay Place.

Things get blurry after that.

More bars, I think. Definitely more drinks. I don't remember the details, obviously. I do remember feeling elated, though. On an entirely different planet. Like nothing could bring me back down to earth.

I have no idea how I ended up here.

'Alcohol poisoning,' Dr Burns fills in for me. 'You fell unconscious and couldn't be roused. Luka called an ambulance for you.'

'Luka's here?' I say.

Dr Burns frowns. 'He only called the ambulance. He didn't come in.' Quickly, she says, 'Do you know how much you had to drink tonight, Zelle?'

I pick up a lock of my hair. It's sticky, and it smells. Jesus. I try to comb out whatever's tangled through it, my fingers tugging out clumps of blue. The dye's starting to fade, and my bleached blonde is showing through.

I eye Dr Burns. What a stupid question. As if I was keeping count.

'Do you really want an answer to that?' I say.

Dr Burns ignores the snark and sits down on the bed, which feels overly familiar for someone I met only five minutes ago. I'm half-expecting her to grab my hand.

'How often do you drink?' she says, trying on a soft voice.

'God, I don't know. No more than anyone else,' I say. It's not like I keep tabs on that, either. Weekends are a given, of course, but we'll do any day depending on who's busy and who's doing what. It's not like school is a priority for me, and Tabitha and Lucy and Anahera and Luka are at uni so their schedules are flexible.

Dr Burns gives me the Suspicious Glare.

'You're still seventeen,' she says.

Big deal. Fake IDs can get you anywhere when you know the right places.

'I'm eighteen in three months,' I say.

'You were lucky your friends called for help when they did,' she says. She enunciates every word, making sure my alcohol-addled brain absorbs it all. 'You had a close call, Zelle. Very close.'

I don't ask her, *Close to what?* It'll be textbook scaremongering for every underager who ends up here on a Saturday night. I don't indulge her.

I think I can guess what she'd tell me anyway.

A new panic seizes me, and I sit up taller. 'You didn't call Mum, did you?'

Dr Burns smiles in a way that I think is supposed to be sympathetic but looks more like a shark getting ready to feast. 'I'm sorry, Zelle,' she says. 'Because you're still a minor, I had no choice. She should be here any minute.'

Oh, fuck me sideways. I lean back on the pillow and close my eyes.

I'm screwed.

I'm completely, totally screwed.

CALLUM

I wake up on The Day with a weight on my stomach.

It's just Descartes, of course: not even deep sleep can avoid feeling *that* monster of a cat. Lately he's taken to sleeping on my bed, which Mum thinks is cute and I think is irritating. God knows how many sleep-ins I've lost after Descartes has decided to start clawing at my face at six in the morning.

Sitting up, I push him away, and he lands on the floor with a thump. He's fifteen now and has arthritis, and his front legs buckle as his body makes impact. He hobbles off and gives me an indignant meow.

'Piss off,' I say.

I'm gifted with a prime view of his arse as he saunters away.

I reach for my phone on the bedside table and check the time. It's 7.15: just under four hours until the interview.

I feel sick.

A careful hand knocks on the door, then Mum walks in. Badger-eyed and bed-headed, she looks like a sad excuse for a zombie in a B-grade sci-fi movie.

'You awake?' she says.

'Unfortunately,' I say.

Descartes walks a lazy circle around her dressing gown. She scoops him up and cradles him. He wriggles in protest.

'Did Descartes wake you up?'

I nod.

'He must know it's a special day.'

'Descartes is a cat, Mum.'

'You could at least humour me, Cal.' Mum plonks him back on the bed. 'Get up,' she says. 'You'll want to leave by nine if you don't want to be late.'

'I know.'

'You'll do great.'

'Uh huh.'

(I don't believe her.)

Mum rips the bedsheets off me. 'Go on. Get ready. I won't feel relaxed until you do.'

'Is that an order?'

'That's an order.'

'Roger that, captain.'

Mum grins, reaches out to pat my shoulder. 'You've worked hard for this,' she says. 'You deserve it.'

'Don't get soppy.'

'Don't get snarky or I'll tell you who your real mother is.' She grins at me and leaves the room. I reach forward and rub Descartes behind the ears.

'I'll be okay, won't I?' I say, nuzzling my face into his.

He swipes a paw across my cheek in response.

Just over half an hour later I'm showered, dressed, and no more ready for today than when I first woke up. Mum's already left for work — I heard her scrabbling for her car keys while I was still in the shower, the harried 'Goodbye, Cal, and good luck!' echoing down the hall. For a clinical psychologist who spends all day helping people achieve *calmness, clarity and wellbeing* (as her website says), my mother lives in a perpetual state of chaos.

Kate's in the kitchen already, splashing milk into two mugs of coffee. This is progress: for the past week and a half, since she moved back home, she hasn't got up before midday.

'Morning,' she says, her voice a singsong. 'I made you breakfast.'

My sister Kate is twenty-two. Until the start of this month she was living a three-hour drive away in Dunedin, doing her Master's (microbiology; she inherited the science gene from Mum) and sharing a loft apartment with Dermott, her Irish boyfriend (also doing his Master's). Everything going swimmingly.

Until they both graduated. And Dermott's visa ran out. Which he decided not to renew. Which made him decide that Kilkenny was a bit far to pull off a long-distance relationship. Which prompted Kate — single, heartbroken and newly an expert in flesh-eating organisms — to enter her quarter-life crisis, leave Dunedin and move back home.

'You're up early,' I say, taking a seat at the table, where Kate presents me with one of the coffee mugs and a plate with two pieces of thickly buttered toast.

'I wanted to see you off before your interview,' she says.

I take a tentative sip of the coffee. I'm all for early-morning caffeine, but right now I feel like a fizzing, wired mess. I push the mug and the plate of toast away.

'I'm not sure I can stomach this.'

'Go on, Cal. Breakfast is the most important meal of the day and all that. And I got out of bed at seven-thirty for this, so at least make me feel like my efforts were worthwhile.'

I have what my mother calls a 'delicate stomach'. To paraphrase: I throw up when I'm nervous. Combine that with an aching shyness and a dose of social anxiety, and cue the montage of embarrassing moments where my grand gestures have taken over the show. Aged nine, about to give a speech in front of my class. Aged thirteen, when I was a groomsman at my cousin Darren's wedding. Last year, just before my final exams. And the year before that.

I take a small bite of toast to appease Kate. It tastes like fireplace ash in my mouth. 'I'll never be accepted if I throw up.'

'First of all, that won't happen. And, if it does, at least give your projectile vomit some substance. Nothing says *prospective journalist* better than chundering all over your interviewers. That'll give you a point of difference.'

I don't laugh.

'I'm joking, Callum.' Kate pulls me into a headlock.

'You're going to be great today,' she says. 'That spot is yours.'

Her hair is pale blonde, a few shades lighter than mine. Wayward strands tickle against my shoulder. I reach around and ruffle her head, sending hair flying. It's been a couple of years now since she swapped her waist-length locks for a short bob crop, but the novelty hasn't worn off.

'Thanks,' I say as she lets me go. We lock eyes and grin. When Kate smiles, it's like a bad case of cold: infectious, annoying, and unavoidably going to spread to you too. I down my coffee in four quick mouthfuls and get up from the table, taking the plate of toast with me. 'I gotta go,' I say. I make my retreat down the hallway.

'You better eat that,' Kate calls after me. 'Oh, and good luck, of course. And don't crash my car.'

(Advantage of Kate moving home: I get to use her car.)

From the safety of my bedroom, I throw the toast into the rose bushes below my open window.

It's just past nine by the time I leave the house. The interview isn't until 10.30, but it's being held in Queenstown, an hour and a half's drive away from here. Welcome to Mistakesville, Central Otago: the absolute middle of nowhere.

Here's everything you need to know about Mistakesville:

1. Okay, so it's not *officially* called Mistakesville.
   It's Stakesville, named after the gold miner who

established this town in the 1860s, William Stakes. (Creativity evidently wasn't his strong suit.) But Stakes's surveying error led to the town being established 10 kilometres south of where it was supposed to be, and there's no good reason why anyone would voluntarily live here.

2. We've clung on to the 'Mistakesville' brand to attract visitors to the town, since nothing else will. We've got enough amenities to be useful — one café, one hotel, one petrol station and one medical centre. Beyond that, all we offer is a meagre smattering of sad shops masquerading as a main street. Our tourist brochures claim that we're *an essential stop on the journey through tracing the history of the Otago gold rush*. In reality, we're a toilet-stop town.

3. The population is 723.

4. I've lived here my entire life. Unfortunately.

The road is winding and empty and I'm grateful for the quiet. The plus side of living in a dead-end town: there's enough solitude for me to freak out in peace.

Eventually I pull up outside the run-down Queenstown Events Centre and, when I've triple-checked that no one's around, close my eyes and take the deepest breath I can. This is one of Mum's many mindfulness techniques. It works. Sometimes.

Today, though, deep breathing doesn't even touch the nervousness that's been growing inside me for months, ever since I first filled out the application forms. A Bachelor of Broadcasting Communications, majoring in journalism. It's been my dream for years, but I applied assuming I'd get nothing more than a polite rejection letter, a brush-off to a deluded dreamer amongst hundreds of others. Then came the *congratulations* email just over three weeks ago, right when I'd begun to lose hope.

The broadcasting school carries out interviews for shortlisted candidates all around the country. A lot of people try out for this thing — including, it seems, enough kids from Central Otago for them to be holding interviews here.

I still can't believe I'm one of them.

When I finally get out of the car and into the waiting room, I've barely got ten minutes before the interview starts. There's a string of messages on my phone: several from the group chat with Fox and Mac, all variations on *good luck you'll do great,* which I swipe away and make a mental reminder to deal with later. I don't have room in my brain for niceties right now.

And then I see the latest notification, a text from an unknown number sent two minutes ago.

My heart freezes.

hey, callum. it's zelle. i know it's been a long time, but i thought you should know that i'm moving back to stakesville. i arrive tonight.

i hope we can talk.

Zelle. Zelle Bachmann.

This can't be happening. This really, really can't be happening.

Zelle Bachmann is back.

Zelle Bachmann is back.

Zelle Bachmann is *back*?

My heart is thundering so hard it feels like a cardiac arrest waiting to happen. My ears ring and my hands shake. Why now? Why, after three years of radio silence?

Why the hell is Zelle Bachmann coming back to our town?

My panic is interrupted by the sound of throat-clearing. I switch off my phone and force myself to look up.

A man is standing in the doorway, looking unimpressed.

'Callum Rig?' he says. 'We're ready for you.'

Oh, God, not now. My breathing's getting heavy. Stomach heaving. All too familiar.

The man's eyebrows furrow.

'You okay, Callum?' he asks.

I lean against the wall, trying to curb the nausea that's creeping up my throat. 'I . . . I just—' I stammer, but before I've formed a proper sentence, this morning's coffee and meagre bites of toast make their grand exit from my stomach to my mouth.

Kate was right. It could've done with some more substance.

The interviewer doesn't react. His eyes slide from my face to the patch of sick on the floor and to the bits of vomit that have sprayed the tips of his shiny black shoes.

I'm beyond embarrassed. I can already feel round two coming on.

'Oh, shit. God. I'm so sorry—'

And I run straight out of the building.

My interview: over. My chance at journalism school: over.

I'm screwed.

I'm completely, totally screwed.

ZELLE

I do *not* have a drinking problem.

Really.

I don't.

Sure, that Saturday two weeks ago went too far, but that's all it was: an accident. It's not like I went into the night *aiming* to wake up in a hospital four hours later attached to an IV drip. A mistake, that's all. And what alcohol-drinking teenager hasn't accidentally gone past their limits before?

And you only need to take one look at me to see that I absolutely, honest-to-God, don't have a problem. People with real problems are fat men in their forties who pass out on the couch with a glass of whiskey in their hands. They're the homeless people who shout at you on the street in the middle of the day.

Luka got me the fake ID. Anahera and I met at high

school, but she's in the year above me, and instead of leaving me behind when she started uni and met Lucy and Tabitha and Luka, she let me join their circle. Having the ID means I'm not left out. It means we can have fun.

I don't have a problem. I don't.

I won't know who I am if I do.

It's after nine, and the road to Stakesville is dark. Turns out Mum wasn't joking when she brought me back from the hospital, when she said we'd be moving back here.

To be honest, I knew we'd have to return someday. I just didn't know that my one-off Saturday night incident would be the reason we did.

'How much longer?' I ask. We've been in the car all day. Began our trip south as soon as we got off the early-morning Picton ferry. I'm not just having cabin fever, I'm having a cabin aneurysm.

Mum's eyes flick to the rear-vision mirror. 'Twenty minutes. You know this road.'

'I need to pee.'

'You can wait twenty minutes.'

Bitch.

Ten minutes pass. The fluorescent-green sign dazzled by our headlights says we're still eight kilometres out from Stakesville.

When we first moved here, I thought the town's nickname was hilarious: *Mistakesville*. Now I realise it's just a town that isn't even supposed to be here. And a town where I'm not supposed to be either.

'Mum,' I say. 'Pee.'

'No.'

'I'm busting.'

'You can hold on.'

I turn to face the window. 'Cow,' I murmur.

'I know I was meant to hear that, Giselle Artemisia Bachmann,' Mum says. I only get the full-name treatment when she's *really* pissed off with me. Which is often.

During the day there's not much to see in Stakesville, but at night it's a full-on ghost town. If it weren't for the flickers of light from the houses in the distance, you wouldn't know anyone lived here at all.

I'm really not ready to come back here.

I check my phone for messages. Callum hasn't replied to my text this morning . Maybe he's changed his number. Maybe he doesn't live here anymore. Maybe I'm blocked. Or maybe he just didn't want to reply. Which is completely and utterly reasonable, so I don't know why I'm still expecting something.

I look at Mum. Try to see if the anxiety that's suffocating me like a second skin is visible on her too. As always, her face is set like stone.

She notices me watching. 'Almost there,' she says.

As if I need reminding.

The Sanctuary isn't in the main part of town but up a country road. Dirt clouds billow behind us as we turn off from the highway up dusty, unsealed gravel. The noise of stones crunching beneath our tyres is so loud, neither of us bothers to speak.

At the end of what's probably the world's longest driveway, The Sanctuary flickers in our headlights. We slow down. The sculptures are all still there: Dad's wire men by the letterbox, and the archway that marks the entrance to the property. One wire figure holds a sign: *Welcome to The Sanctuary. Art Gallery & Studio.*

My stomach twists.

Mum stops the car. We're right outside. The house is coated in darkness; of course, the power isn't connected. It's been three years since anyone went near this place.

'We're here,' Mum says.

'I can see that,' I reply.

She hands me a rusted key. 'You pee,' she says. 'I'll unpack the car.'

While Mum busies herself with unloading, I cross the gravel and slip the key into the front door. The bathroom is directly to the left. I walk straight to it, my phone torch pointed at the ground.

And I scream.

There are ants. Everywhere. Swimming *in the toilet bowl.*

For good measure, I scream again.

Mum comes running, but as soon as she sees what I'm staring at, she merely folds her arms. 'Is that it?'

'I can't pee in that!' I shout, gesturing at the toilet. 'It's ant soup.'

'They'll drown when you flush. Big deal. I'll call the plumber on Monday. Or ant exterminator. Whoever.'

Monday. Three nights away. Three nights of peeing on a colony of ants.

'I am *not* using that toilet.'

'It's the only one in the house.'

'It's disgusting.'

'Pee outside, then, if it bothers you that much.'

'Why did we have to come back here?' I scream, trying to hold back tears, and failing. Now that I'm really looking, I'm seeing it's more than just ants: the whole place is a mess. Dust clumps as big as furballs are coughed up in corners of the floor; spiderwebs are hanging from the ceiling, and God knows what else is crawling through the walls. Not to mention our furniture, aching from years without use, and the cluttered old gallery and studio filled with all the stuff we couldn't take with us. Seeing the state of our house, maybe Mum will finally come to her senses. Realise what she's done. Take us back to Wellington.

Her expression doesn't change.

'You know why we're here, Zelle,' she says. 'You drink too much. You're failing school. Your friends are a bad influence. We're here so you can get your life back on track.'

'My life is tracking along just fine,' I spit through gritted teeth. 'School isn't your problem. My friends aren't bad for me. And I don't have a *fucking drinking problem*!'

We glower at each other.

'Don't shout at me,' Mum says.

'I hate this place,' I say. 'And I hate you!'

And then I run outside. I run all the way to the trees at the very edge of the property, far away from the house, from Dad's sculptures, from Mum. I kick at the trunk of a pine tree and throw dirt in the air.

But, damn, I do need to pee.

And I guess I don't really have a choice now.

Even though I've been holding it in for hours, my bladder refuses to let loose on the ground. I squat until my knees ache, and it feels like forever before I achieve anything more than a thin, reluctant trickle. No one can see me out here, but my cheeks blaze anyway. This whole situation is humiliating. Just this morning we were in our cosy penthouse on The Terrace. Screw Dr Burns and her need to blab about my tiny little incident. Screw Mum and her decision to send me to alcohol-free exile.

I could really use a drink right now.

When my toilet ordeal's over, I call Luka. One advantage of The Sanctuary: at least the nearest cellphone tower's close.

My phone rings and rings, and by the time Luka's husky voice comes on the line I'm already crying again.

'Oh . . . hey.' Luka sounds surprised and kind of slow. I'd say he almost sounded sleepy, but I know for a fact that Luka is perpetually nocturnal, and there's no way my call will have woken him up. I've only known him since March, but he's already one of my closest friends. Or something more. I think. I hope.

'Luka,' I sob. 'I hate this. I hate being here. I want to go back to Wellington. This isn't fair.'

'Shh, Zelle,' he says. 'It's okay.'

'No, it's not okay! It's nowhere near okay! I'm stuck in this shithole town for the next three months and I don't even get to see you!'

'You will,' he says, and the complete lack of hesitation in his voice is enough for me to stop crying. I wipe my nose on my sleeve, leaving my hoodie with an impressive smear of clear wet goo. Gross.

'It was an accident,' I mumble.

There's a jumble of indiscernible sounds in the white-noise background, like maybe Luka's walking out of the room. 'I know,' he says.

'I shouldn't have to be here.'

'It's only for a few months,' he says. 'You're eighteen soon. Just a few months until you're old enough to do what you want.'

'A few more months isn't soon enough.'

'Look, Zelle, I'll talk to you tomorrow, okay? I've got an assignment due tomorrow that I've barely started.'

'Okay,' I say, disappointed the call's ending already. 'Bye, Luka.'

'Bye, Zelle,' he says, and hangs up.

I stare down at my now-silent phone. The tears that Luka had helped to stop come falling down my cheeks again. But I'm determined not to be desperate. Only three more months until I turn eighteen. Three months isn't a long time. I can wait. I can be patient. I'll have to be.

It's cold, but I'm determined not to go back inside the house. I'll spend the whole night out here if I have to. If there's one thing I'm good at, it's never admitting defeat. I throw my phone down, pull my knees close to my chest, and try to draw warmth out of my own body.

Luka knows that I used to live in a small town called Stakesville and that we moved away when I was fourteen. He knows we left after my parents broke up. He doesn't know that I had a best friend called Callum and a friend called Fox and a friend called Mac and a friend called Eli and that everyone called us the Famous Five. He doesn't know what happened the summer we moved away.

There's so much here that's buried in the past. And buried it should stay.

I close my eyes, but of course I can't fall asleep under these cold, creaking trees. I wait it out for an hour or so, then slip in through the back door of the house — unlocked for my return — and creep down the hallway to my old bedroom, crawling into a freshly made bed that no longer feels like mine.

CALLUM

Here's everything you need to know about Zelle Bachmann:

1. Her mother is Dutch and her father is German. She can speak both languages, plus French, plus Spanish. And English, of course.

2. She was born in Berlin and came to Stakesville when she was nine. Before that, she'd lived in Brussels, and Paris, and Barcelona. Hence the language skills.

3. Her parents are artists. Famous ones. Hence the globetrotting. Plus the fact that they're probably the richest and most interesting family that Mistakesville's ever had. (And the closest we ever got to dropping the *Mis–*.) The art studio and gallery they operated

on their property was known throughout the country back before they broke up.

4. We were best friends since the day she first arrived.

5. We haven't talked since the day she left, three years and five months ago. The summer we turned fourteen.

6. And now, for no apparent reason, she's back.

After the disaster that was my one and only shot at landing the future of my dreams, I arrive home in a Zelle-shock haze. It was all I could think about on the long drive home. It's a miracle I made it without careening over the centre line and plunging into the Kawarau Gorge.

'So,' Kate says before I've even fully closed the front door, 'how did it go?' She and Mum are standing in the hallway, their smiles on high beam. Here's what I hate about having high expectations placed on you: you have further to fall when you fail.

I'm certain my defeat's obvious: vomit on my breath, vomit on my shirt, *Zelle Bachmann is coming back and I am LOSING IT* written in the worry lines on my forehead. I surreptitiously check my clothing for any incriminating stains while I plaster on my best, fakest smile. 'It was good. Really good, actually.'

'I knew it!' Mum wraps me up in a bear hug, and Kate joins in. 'I'm so proud of you, Cal. Keri will be thrilled with you.'

Keri is my boss at the *Stakesville Chronicle*, the biweekly paper that's the closest thing our town has to a news outlet. I've been a staff writer at the paper for over a year, an over-eager media nerd wanting to get stuck into the job. Keri's the one who first told me about broadcasting school.

She'll be thrilled, all right.

I wrestle my family's arms off me. 'All right,' I say. 'Enough of the paparazzi.' I force out a laugh from the hollowest place inside me.

'I'll make pizza,' Mum says. (There's no such thing as ordering pizza in small-town Central Otago.)

'Brilliant,' I say.

She must be lying.

Surely.

Right?

A cunning plan to test whether I'd respond to her. Her dramatic way of wanting to talk. It's extreme, but likely. Zelle always did everything in extremes.

I'd forgotten how exhausting Zelle Bachmann can be.

My fingers hover over the keyboard, thinking of what to reply. What *do* you say to your former best friend who you haven't seen in over three years? Okay? Sounds good? Welcome back? Fuck off?

Sick of staring at Zelle's name on my screen, I open up my phone gallery to find my photos of Eli.

I don't keep any physical photos of him in my room, even though most people would. I think about him when I want to think about him. It feels too public, too abrasive, to have him staring from my wall or in a frame on my bookshelf. On my phone, it's private. Special. Mine.

In this one it's Eli's fourteenth birthday party. Back when the Famous Five were still together. Eli's grinning, holding up the blue-tongued skink his parents gave him for his birthday. The skink's scaly green skin is the same colour as Eli's eyes. He named it Pablo.

('As in Picasso?' I asked.)

('As in Escobar,' he said.)

That's what prompts me to open up Instagram and send Eli a direct message, even though his account's been deactivated for years.

I am in the shit, dude. DEEP shit.

I don't know what to do.

Hope pablo escobar's doing well btw.

The skink that is. not the drug lord.

I decide I don't have the courage to message Zelle. I wouldn't trust her answer anyway.

There's only one way I can find out the truth for sure.

Kate is curled up on the living-room couch, wrapped in a blanket and watching Netflix. Mum's in her bedroom, either meditating or writing in her gratitude journal or reading some scholarly article on the latest breakthroughs in clinical psychology.

'Can I use your car?' I ask Kate.

'What for?' she asks.

'I don't know. To drive it, maybe?'

She rolls her eyes. 'I meant *where*, idiot.'

'I don't know. Just around.'

'Just around?'

'Need to clear my head.'

'Was driving to Queenstown and back not enough?'

Living with Kate is like living with a member of the Spanish Inquisition.

'Wasn't exactly head-clearing.'

She huffs, not taking her eyes from the TV screen. 'Keys are on the bench. Don't stay out too late. Mum'll get worried.'

'You're the best,' I say.

'Yeah, yeah. Can I get back to my show, please?'

I slip out of the house before she can interrogate me any more.

I know the route to Zelle's place as well as the drive to my own. We practically lived at each other's houses when we were kids; Mum said it was like having a third child, which always made Zelle glow with pleasure.

My hands tighten their grip on the steering wheel as I inch further down the driveway to The Sanctuary. It's a bit suspicious to be 'accidentally' driving down what's clearly a private road, but people get lost round here all the time. It's hard not to, when Stakesville's layout is like an Escher maze.

I slow down to a crawl and turn off my lights. I check the time on the dashboard. It's just after ten. I'm not enough of an idiot to drive all the way down to the gate, so I edge the car off the road and into the grass about a hundred metres away. The slight rise of the road means I can't see over the lip of the hill to the house. I get out and sneak through the knee-length grass, feeling like a child playing cops and robbers. I keep my phone torch pointed to the ground.

My heart speeds up the closer I get. Soon my hands are shaking so hard my torch twitches like strobe lights. My chest tightens, and a brick in my stomach that feels uncomfortably like the one I felt this morning grows heavier.

A few metres shy of reaching the top of the hill, I freeze.

All I have to do is look over. Find out whether she's really here.

But I realise I don't want to know.

Not now.

Not yet.

I'm running back to the car before my brain even makes the conscious decision to move. I throw the door open, crash into the front seat and wrench the keys in the ignition until the engine rumbles into life. I screech off down the road and make the usual five-minute journey back to my house in three. I spend a few minutes sitting in the car, catching my breath and recovering from the whiplash.

I get Zelle's message back up again. And then I press *delete*.

ZELLE

I spend the weekend in hiding.

The furthest I venture from The Sanctuary is to the front gate. Mum braves the crisp Saturday morning to head to the Four Square and comes back with food and a mountain of cleaning supplies. I'm forced to spend the rest of the weekend scrubbing, dusting and washing away three years' worth of grime. At least we manage to get the power re-connected. If this is meant to be some kind of rehab in a country idyll, it sucks.

The only other upside of our weekend cleaning fest is that it gives me an excuse not to face the outside world. Mum doesn't even question why I don't leave the house.

My luck runs out quickly, though.

On Monday morning I'm woken to the sound of opening curtains. Sunlight floods my room, and from the foggy state of my head I can tell it's still far too early to be awake.

'Get up,' Mum says, ripping off my duvet. 'School.'

'What?'

'It's Monday. You have school.'

'You never mentioned *school*!'

'I thought it was obvious. We came here for you to re-establish yourself, not to have a holiday.'

'Oh, no,' I say. 'No, no, no, no, no.'

I can't go to school. Everyone I know will be there.

Callum will be there.

We were always the Famous Five: me, Cal, Mac, Fox and Eli, though of course me and Cal were the closest. We did everything together. I thought we'd be friends for life.

And then Eli wasn't there anymore. And then I wasn't there anymore. And the Famous Five would never exist again.

I'm not ready to face that.

'I'm not even enrolled,' I protest.

'I called the school last week. They've got a place for you.'

'Well, I'm not going.'

'Yes, you are.'

'You can't make me. I'm seventeen. I can drop out.'

'Not while you live with me,' Mum says. It sounds like she's rehearsed these lines a hundred times over.

'Then I'll move out,' I say.

'And how are you going to do that?' Her arms crossed, Mum taps her black-painted fingernails against her upper arms. 'Without any money? Without a car? Without a licence?'

She's got me there. The words are acidic but true. I've never had a job; the amount of money I *do* have wouldn't even buy me a plane ticket to Wellington. I don't know how to drive. I don't even have my learner licence.

I'm stuck.

'I'll get a job,' I say. 'You can't stop me from anything. It's not like I *want* to live with you.'

Mum doesn't respond. Not just because I've said things like this so often it's a waste of time her getting mad. She doesn't respond because deep down, I suspect, my mother wishes the same too.

I leap out of bed, grab a bundle of clothes and head for the hallway.

'Where are you going?' Mum says.

I don't reply.

'Giselle,' she calls. 'Giselle, come back.'

But I don't listen as I slam the back door.

I get changed in the trees behind the house. Mum doesn't try to find me, which is usually how it goes. We'll fight, I'll storm off and stay with Luka or Anahera or whoever else can have me over, return home when I feel ready to face her, pretend that nothing happened, and wait for the next argument to ensue. Luka once said it's strange that my mum never comes after me. He doesn't understand that it's easier this way.

Hastily dressed, I sneak out into the early-morning sunlight and through the front gate. I walk down the driveway, past Dad's stupid sculptures, and head onto the road that leads into town.

As I go, I formulate an escape plan. If I want to get out of here, I need a job. I don't need to graduate Year Thirteen: I barely go to school as it is. Once I have money, nothing will stop me. I'm not sure where I'll find work, given that Stakesville's economy isn't exactly booming. But the one thing I know for sure is that I absolutely can't stay here.

It's a clear, bright morning, the surrounding hills dappled in gold. Above them glimmer the mountain peaks, snowless until the next cold snap. We moved here when Dad was going through his painting phase. I think he fancied himself the next Monet or something. Mum and Dad had done well enough in Europe that they used the money they'd earned to buy the old farmhouse villa that became The Sanctuary. Stakesville was Dad's muse. He loved it. We all did.

At first, that is.

I pick up my speed. Half-formed shapes on the horizon grow to solid houses, and soon I'm on the outskirts of town. Mrs Godfrey's house is still painted ghastly yellow; the Catholic church's paddock is still filled with sheep; the corner dairy still advertises its $2 hot chips. It feels like I've stepped back in time, that I've walked straight into a world where I'm fourteen again.

I really haven't missed this place.

I decide to start my job search on the main road. I'm careful to avoid the west side of town: that's where the school is, and where Callum's house is too. Provided he still lives there. His radio silence isn't helping.

I try the second-hand store first, in large part because it's the only thing that's open this early in the day. Nicky McAllister likes to call Nicky's Knick Knacks an antique store, but everyone knows it's just a glorified rubbish dump for our town's unwanted possessions. The business doesn't do too badly, considering Nicky's owned the place for as long as I can remember. Me and Cal used to ride our bikes to her store on Saturdays. She'd give us homemade shortbread and let us walk her gentle old terrier, Biscuit. Nicky's batshit crazy, but she's the heart of the town. She'll know where I'll be able to find work.

The ping of the bell above the shop door sounds just like childhood. It's the chorus of summer days and shortbread, fresh-cut grass and tyre marks. Nicky, spindly as ever, is sitting at the front counter. There's no sign of Biscuit.

'Morning,' she says. Then she looks up. 'Heaven's below, is that you, Zelle?'

I fight the urge to run away as Nicky approaches. 'Look at you,' she says, wrapping me into a hug. It's like being strangled by a stick. 'What are you doing here? When'd you come back? And what's wrong with your hair?'

I push my hair behind my ears, choosing not to answer the last question. 'We got here a couple of days ago,' I say. 'We're just refurbishing The Sanctuary.' At least this is true. 'We're only here for a couple of months.' This, I hope, is true too. Before she can ask any more questions, I jump in. 'How are you? How's the business?'

'Oh, you know. Same day, different shit.'

'Don't you mean same shit, different—'

'Look at these!' Nicky interrupts, gesturing at a collection of glass figurines on the counter. 'These were donated yesterday by the ladies from the croquet society. They're hideous! Who on the Devil's green earth would want these?'

'They are a bit—'

'One woman's treasure is another woman's trash. Honestly, Zelle. Anyway. What's a young lass like you wanting to talk to me for? Shouldn't you be in school? Or is that not a thing your generation does anymore?'

I shrug, deciding that's another question I don't want to answer. I gaze over the counter to where the dog bed always sat. 'Where's Biscuit?' I ask.

Nicky's lips twist into a frown. 'Ach, you poor lassie. You really haven't been here for a long time, have you? Biscuit died a couple of years ago. Tumour on her heart.'

'Oh—' A strange lump rises in my throat. 'I'm sorry.'

'Don't be,' she says. 'She was a good dog but a pain in the beehive, you know? I'm enjoying the single life.' She laughs. 'Anyway. What are you here for?'

'Well . . . since we're going to be here a while, I'm hoping to find a job. I was wondering if you knew of anything?'

'Funny you asked,' Nicky says. 'I've been struggling to keep up with managing the store on my lonesome lately. One hip in the grave and all that.' She grins, still the same maniacal smile with three of her front teeth missing. Cal and I used to joke about finding her teeth for sale in the shop. 'Plus, I could do with some company. What do you say, lassie?'

A job with Nicky McAllister. Spending my days holed up with a fruitcake of a woman in a store that smells like wet socks and death.

I can't think of anything worse.

'I don't know,' I say.

'Come on, lassie. I don't bite.' Nicky's laugh conjures up images of hook-nosed witches with black hats and broomsticks. She flings out her arms. 'It's not like Stakesville's bursting with opportunities, anyway.'

'Will you pay me?'

Nicky rolls her eyes. 'Good lord, what happened to working out of the kindness of your heart? Yes, I'll pay you. I've got a neat collection of shillings and pennies. Edwardian era. Mint condition.'

I'm gaping like a fish. 'I meant real—'

'I'm joking, lassie.' She toddles back behind the counter and stabs a finger at the figurines. 'Right. How about you put some price labels on these monstrosities and get them out of my sight?'

'You want me to start, like, right now?'

'No time like the present. I'll show you where the pricing gun is. Come on, lassie. Get that A into G.'

It's going to be a long day.

CALLUM

'Well, well, well,' Fox says on Monday morning. 'How'd the interview go, soldier?'

He and Mac are waiting at our usual spot on the way to school. They both live in the south side of town, and I live in the west, which also happens to be where school is. Our routes meet at the intersection just before the final block. We've been meeting each other at this point since we were old enough to walk to school on our own.

'It was fine,' I say. 'Good, I think.'

There's a silence which indicates I'm expected to elaborate, but I don't.

'And?' Mac says. 'Don't leave us hanging. Do you think you got in?'

'I don't know,' I say. Of all the lies I've told about the interview, this one's the closest to the truth. 'There's a lot of competition. It's out of my hands now.'

'Well,' Mac says, '*when* you get in, which you totally will, we'll go out for dinner.'

'As long as you pay,' Fox adds, nudging me with his elbow.

I roll my eyes. 'Always so generous.'

'Only the best for our friends,' Fox and Mac say in unison. (A lot of people mistake Fox and Mac for twins. They're not even related, but with the way they speak over each other and the fact they've been neighbours their whole lives, even I sometimes forget.)

Our banter is the perfect segue back to our usual before-school routine: laughing, joking, teasing. I'm grateful not to be talking about the interview.

But there's something else on my mind.

Stakesville Area School has one hundred and twelve students, from first-year primary to the seventeen of us Year Thirteens. Eighteen, if Zelle makes an appearance.

As the school gates get closer, I'm constantly checking out the students humming around the entrance. Looking for her.

I don't know whether to be relieved or not when every short, freckly girl with dirt-blonde hair I spot turns out not to be Zelle.

'Callum.' Fox waves a hand in front of my face. 'Are you there?'

'Sorry?'

'What's up with you? You're spacing out.'

'I'm fine.' I blink my eyes furiously, trying to shake myself back into the present. 'Just . . . tired.'

I know I should tell Mac and Fox about the text from Zelle. But I've already deleted the message, and besides, if it turns out to be a lie, what would be the point in saying anything? The last thing any of us need, or want, is to have a Zelle-sized bomb dropped on our lives. Which inevitably is also an Eli-sized bomb.

I lead the way to our first class together, maths. It's exactly half-past, so everyone's here already. Fourteen sets of eyes look up as I swing open the door.

Zelle isn't here.

We head over to our usual table in the corner, and I try to relax now it's looking likely there'll be no run-ins with her today. It's a couple of minutes before Mr Abassi waddles in, holding his mug that says *Maths puns are the first SINE of madness*. A mug that should be illegal.

'What's everyone looking so morose for?' he says. 'It's first period on a Monday. And we're doing trigonometry.'

There's a collective groan.

'And,' Mr Abassi adds, 'we've got a new person joining the class today.'

'Oh, shit.'

Mac's brow furrows. 'What?' she says.

I have a vision of myself vomiting on the table as Zelle walks in. My palms grow sweaty, and I want to run away.

It's exactly the same as when I was nine years old and met Zelle for the first time. It was a Wednesday, and it was June, and it was the fifth week of term. Zelle was walking in with her parents. I remember thinking that it was a pretty weird time to be the new kid: in the middle of the term, in the middle of the year, in the middle of the week. Her family looked pretty weird, too. Obviously not from around here. Zelle's mum was all in black as though dressed for a funeral. Her dad had on this ill-fitting suit and looked bored out of his mind. Zelle had obviously been forced into an expensive-looking dress for the occasion, and I could tell she'd have rather been seen dead than in that outfit. Her hair flowed wild and ragged and her shoes were caked in mud. Below the hem of her dress were two dirty knees.

Everyone stared at Zelle, and I did too, but she just stared right back. Even then, I knew she had the sort of confidence I could only dream of.

I've never been the type of person to draw people in. I already had Fox and Mac and Eli as friends, but only because they came to me first, rescued me from my chronic shyness. But that day, out of all the kids in the classroom, Zelle met my eyes and walked over to me.

'Look,' she said, unfurling her fist. A small, metallic-blue insect crawled out. 'It's a steelblue ladybird. I've never seen one before.' She spoke fast and urgently and with a strange accent. 'Let's make a home for it,' she said.

And we did. The ladybird didn't last the day: we cut too-big holes in the paper box we crafted, and the bug crawled out. But that didn't matter, because Zelle already felt like my best friend and everything else seemed irrelevant.

Mac nudges my elbow. 'Cal?' she says.

I swallow. 'I think, uh, I think that—'

'And here we are,' Mr Abassi says. 'A few minutes late,

but better late than never. Class, Finn. Finn, class. I won't force you through any more introductions, Mr Nassar. Take a seat. Trigonometry awaits.'

I stop. I turn my head. I look up.

It's not her.

It's not her.

It's not Zelle.

The boy — Finn — is tall and slightly awkward, like his limbs don't know how to work together. He has black hair parted down the middle, and thick lashes and olive skin. He wears pants and a shirt in a style that's way chicer than anyone else in Mistakesville. The class gapes at this mystery new boy, but he doesn't seem fazed. If I had a classroom full of teenagers staring at me, I would be a melted heap on the floor.

He looks over at our corner. Our eyes lock. The smallest hint of a smile edges up the corner of his lips.

He walks over.

He pulls out a chair and sits next to me.

'Now, let's explore the wonderful world of inverse trigonometric functions,' Mr Abassi announces before Finn even gets a chance to say hello.

Mr Abassi's waffle sounds like slush in my ears. Mac pokes my arm with her pencil.

'What were you saying before?' she whispers.

Fox watches. I'm acutely aware that Finn is watching too.

'Doesn't matter.'

'It seemed important.'

I flap my hand, as if swatting away a fly. 'I'll tell you later.'

My cheeks flame. Finn is listening to every word I say.

When Mr Abassi waves us off to have a group discussion about triangles, Mac pounces. She's an extrovert, a different species.

'Hey,' she says to Finn. 'I'm Mac. This is Fox' (she points at Fox), 'and that's Callum' (she points at me). 'Where are you from?'

'Alexandra,' Finn says.

I can tell we're all thinking the same thing. This boy has townie energy. He's too cool to be from small-town Central Otago. I mean, compared to Mistakesville, Alex is like Disneyland (it actually has a proper supermarket), but it's hardly anywhere impressive. 'My dad's a doctor,' Finn continues. 'He got a job at the medical centre.'

So the new boy is cool, confident *and* rich. Typical.

'Where do you live?' Mac says.

'Down on Smyth Street. Right at the end.'

'No way,' Mac says. 'Cal lives on Smyth, too. Don't you, Cal?'

'Last time I checked,' I say, and make a studious effort not to reciprocate Finn's eye contact.

'Maybe you can show me around,' he says.

I shrug. 'Really isn't much to see. There's a reason why we call this place *Mis*takesville.'

Which is a perfect way of killing a conversation. Which is kind of what I intended.

Mac glares at me, then turns back to Finn, rescuing

the conversation before it gets too awkward. Finn is easy-going, affable. Talks even more than Mac does. Laughs a lot, and makes the others laugh, and even coaxes Fox into being chattier than usual. By the end of the period, they're practically best friends. I've barely spoken at all.

While I'm reaching for my backpack, I sense Finn's presence behind me.

'What class have you got now?' he asks.

'Media studies,' I say, swinging my bag over my shoulder. Then, figuring I owe him a bit of effort: 'You?'

'Chemistry,' he says. He almost looks disappointed. Which is weird. 'I'll see you later, then.'

'See you later,' I say, deliberately looking at just Fox and Mac.

I practically run out the classroom door.

ZELLE

The biggest surprise on my first day of working at Nicky's Knick Knacks is how much there is to *do*.

It turns out that running a second-hand store is a real business. There're items to sort through, collections to tidy, customers to deal with. Even when it seems like there's nothing to do, Nicky always finds me something. By midday I'm shattered.

I can't say I'm enjoying it, exactly.

At half twelve Nicky presses a twenty-dollar note into my hand and waves me off. 'Go take half an hour and sit in the sun,' she says. 'Buy yourself something to eat.'

I walk into the Four Square, Stakesville's pathetic excuse for a supermarket, keeping my head down the entire time. I snag the first sandwich I can find and don't make eye contact with Brenda Donohue as I wait at her till. Of course, the town's too archaic for self-checkout machines.

Brenda must be one of the oldest checkout operators in the country, so I'm hoping she won't remember or recognise me, especially with my hair.

But she does. 'You look familiar,' she says, passing over my change. 'Local?'

'No,' I say. 'Just passing through.'

She squints. 'Are you sure?'

'One hundred percent.'

'Well, you are the spitting image of—'

'Sorry,' I interrupt. 'I have to go. Thanks!' I take the sandwich and head back to Nicky's store.

Mum's BMW is parked outside. Fuck me sideways.

I think about turning around and running back to The Sanctuary, just to stretch out my freedom a little bit longer. But I know that running is futile. I take a deep breath, prepare myself for the shitstorm, and open the door.

It's not the scene I'm expecting. Nicky and my mother are sitting at the small table in the corner of the shop, a pot of tea and two mismatched cups between them. Mum is *laughing*. Nicky is making my mother *laugh*. My mother, who's about as likely to laugh as a brick wall.

'Hello, lassie,' Nicky says. 'Sit down. Tea?'

I'm so bewildered I don't even speak, and take a seat at the table like an obedient puppy. Nicky pours tea into a chipped polka-dot mug. I can't look at my mother.

'So you *were* supposed to be in school,' Nicky says, while I sip the tea and stare at the table. I look up, expecting her to be angry, but she just seems bemused. 'Your mother was worried.'

'How did you find me?' I say, finally meeting Mum's eyes.

'I figured you'd probably gone into town. I called Nicky first. I thought she'd be likely to know.'

At least my mum and I think the same on some things.

'Anneke and I have been having a good chat,' Nicky says. 'You're a bit off the tracks, aren't you lassie?'

I snap my head towards Mum. 'What have you been talking about?' I say, knowing she'll understand what I mean. If she's told Nicky about why we left Wellington, about me—

'I know you're not a fan of school,' Mum says. 'But while we're back here renovating the house, you need to keep up your education. It's your final year of school, Zelle. You can't waste it.'

I look at Nicky, trying to read her face to see whether Mum has told her a different story — the truth. But she just nods along, and she's transparent enough that I know this is the same story Mum told her too.

My shoulders melt with relief.

'We've got a proposal for you, though,' Nicky says. 'We think it'd be a good thing for you to work. Teach you commitment and independence and whatnot. So, the deal is, I'll give you a weekend shift at the shop if you go to school.' She leans back in her chair. 'What do you say, lassie?'

I study them both. It feels like I'm being parented. And that is not something I'm used to.

'When do I have to start?'

'Tomorrow,' Mum says.

'Next week.'

'Tomorrow, Zelle.'

'Next week, or I won't go.'

The first flicker of anger ignites. '*Ik waarschuw je—*'

'How much would you learn in one week of school?' Nicky asks me.

I shrug. 'Fuck all.'

'*Giselle.*'

'This week you can work full time in the shop,' Nicky says, ignoring Mum's agitation. 'Next week you can go back to school. The real world can teach you just as much as school can.' She raises her eyebrows. 'But only if that's okay with Anneke, of course.'

Mum sighs. 'I suppose so,' she huffs. 'But only if you promise you'll *definitely* go next week.'

'Ditto,' Nicky says. 'That's the one condition of this deal.'

'Fine,' I say. 'I'll work here for the rest of the week. And I'll go back to school next week.'

It's not ideal, but at least I don't have to worry about it for now. I'm spared from any run-ins with Cal, or Fox, or Mac. I'll have time to think. To prepare.

'Good lassie,' Nicky says. 'Now, back to work.'

Mum stands up from the table. 'I'll be back here to pick you up at four,' she says. Turning to Nicky, she adds, 'Thank you,' her voice swelled with more emotion than I've heard from her for years.

Nicky gives her a quick hug. 'Good luck with your

renovations. It must be difficult without Walter.'

Mum smiles carefully. She's a master at hiding her feelings, but the sadness in her eyes whenever Dad gets mentioned is one she can never control.

As promised, Mum comes back to collect me at four.

'Good day?' she asks.

'Yep,' I say.

When we're not fighting, this is the usual extent of our conversation.

As she starts the car, I get out my phone to send a message to Luka.

I got a job and it's not entirely shit!!!!

miss you tho

I can tell by the small green circle in the corner of Luka's profile picture that he's online. I wait for him to reply: he's usually pretty quick. But my message remains on delivered. Eventually, Luka's green circle disappears. I click out and onto my group chat with Tabitha, Lucy and Anahera — the friends I was with that Saturday night in Wellington.

guess what . . . I got a job!! I type.

I don't wait to see who's online. I turn off my phone, gaze out the window, and say nothing as Mum drives us home.

CALLUM

I make it to 8.15 on Tuesday morning before my world is turned upside down.

Again.

'Who's that waiting outside?' Mum says, just as I'm bending over to tie my Converse. I look up.

It's Finn.

'He looks new. Is he new?'

'Uh huh,' I say. 'Okay. Gotta go. Bye.'

I bolt out the door.

The thing about Finn is he looks completely at ease waiting on the street, as if it's not awkward at all, as if we've been doing this for years and he hasn't lived here five minutes and I've never even told him which house is mine.

'Hey,' he says. Chin raise. Eyebrow raise. Effortless. His hair is extra-floppy today, and it bounces with the bop of his head.

'Uh,' I say.

His smirk is bemused. 'I spent last night knocking on all the doors along Smyth Street asking which house was yours. Since you were wondering.'

'You . . . did?'

'No,' Finn says. His laugh echoes down the street. 'I asked Mac where you lived. I didn't trust myself to find the right way to school on my own. My dad dropped me off yesterday morning. But his sense of direction's pretty terrible, and he's even more hopeless at using Google Maps, which is why I ended up being so late.'

At least his filling-in of the silence means I don't have to do it.

Finn walks the tiniest bit ahead of me. His backpack is forest green. He has a Pride badge pinned on the front pocket.

'How long have you been friends with Fox and Mac?' he asks, turning on his heels and walking backwards. My face flushes. His eye contact is intimidating.

'My whole life, pretty much.' I shrug. 'That's how it goes in small towns.'

(Which you would already know, I add to myself.)

'Has it always been just the three of you?'

Oh God. Bringing up Eli and Zelle is the last thing I want to do right now. Or ever.

I wave a hand dismissively. 'Friends come and go. We've always been the tightest.'

It feels like an insult to shrug off our history like this, but there'd be no simple way to explain the Famous Five and its downfall without an hours-long monologue. Besides, since that summer three years ago Mac, Fox and I have mostly stuck to ourselves.

'Cute,' Finn says. He does a little skip. 'What are you doing after school today?'

(WHY DOES HE WANT TO KNOW?)

'I'm hoping you'll be my chaperone for the way home.'

(Is that the first hint of shyness in his smile?)

'Sorry,' I say. 'You'll have to find a replacement. I have work.'

'Where do you work?'

He'd get along well with Kate, I think. Two relentless interrogators.

'I write for the *Stakesville Chronicle*.' I hate talking about work. 'It's, like, the town newspaper.'

'No way. Really? So you're a writer?'

'I guess so?'

'Is that what you're gonna study at uni?'

I'm saved from giving an answer by Fox and Mac waving from our usual meeting spot.

Thank God.

'Hey,' Mac says. 'Look at you two. Best buds already.'

I hope she doesn't see how I blush.

I arrive at the town's only café at 3.15. Tim Cooney's already there, talking to an elderly lady who looks completely starstruck. In Mistakesville, Tim Cooney is about the closest thing we have to a celebrity. He's the town's representative on the regional council and is standing against two other candidates for re-election next month. Keri, my boss and chief editor at the *Stakesville Chronicle*, has tasked me with doing a profile on him.

'You must be Callum,' he says, shooing his admirer away, and extending a hand. 'Lovely to meet you. Let me grab you a coffee.'

I don't decline: I know Tim Cooney's rich enough to splurge five dollars on a junior reporter. He swaggers back to the table a couple of minutes later, adjusting his tie. (He's wearing a suit. I *know*.)

It goes unspoken that we're not starting the interview straight away, so Tim Cooney makes small talk while we wait for our coffees to arrive. He asks me all the usual things while I fire up my laptop, loading up my list of questions and my recording app: how's school, what am I doing after I finish, what are my career aspirations, where do I see myself in five years, etc, etc. I reply mechanically, sourcing my responses from the part of my brain that's memorised how to answer the questions that adults always ask seventeen-going-on-eighteen-year-olds. School's fine, I'm applying to broadcasting school, I'm hoping one day I'll work somewhere in the media, etc, etc.

I'm saved from the monotony when Martin arrives with our coffees. I like Martin. He and his partner Hugo arrived in town and opened up the café about a year ago — while *revolutionised* isn't quite the word, they've injected some much-needed new life into the town. He smiles and says hello, as he always does.

'Never much liked that guy, to be honest,' Tim Cooney

mutters, once Martin's out of earshot.

I stir my flat white and take a sip. (Martin makes the best coffees.) 'Why's that?' I say. I keep my voice level.

'Oh, you know.' Tim Cooney does an exaggerated flap of his hand, which is obviously meant to signal *gay*. 'Very camp, isn't he?'

I try my hardest not to react, even though my heart has hitched up a notch and my face feels hot with anger. Why does he think this is something worth saying? Why does he think this at all?

'You don't like that?' I ask, my tone neutral. Curious. Journalistically objective. *Don't burn your sources,* I can hear Keri whisper in my ear.

'Everyone should have the freedom to do as they please,' Tim Cooney says, which doesn't really answer my question, which probably means that what he really thinks is no. 'But there's no need to . . . you know. Show off about it. Stick it in everyone's faces.'

I keep my eyes on my flat white. It's too embarrassing to make eye contact with Tim Cooney while he says this.

'He's just being himself, though, isn't he?' I say. (Neutral. Curious. Journalistically objective.)

Tim Cooney looks back over his shoulder. Martin's at the coffee machine, smiling as he always does, humming along to the song playing through the speakers.

'Hm,' he says. 'Is he?' He pulls down the cuffs of his sleeves. 'Anyway. Shall we get on with the interview?'

And thus begin almost forty-five minutes of Tim Cooney's sales pitch about why he is the most suitable middle-aged, bald, white man to be serving our community, citing all the things he's achieved (an upgrade to the Stakesville tourist information centre, better carparking on the main road, a new community playground), and the issues our town still faces (like a declining local economy that means not even a flash new information centre can convince tourists to spend their money on us). Now that he's on the record, nothing homophobic or otherwise controversial comes out of his mouth: it's all smiles, business, passion and vision for our little corner of Central Otago.

I barely listen, asking my questions from the screen in front of me and letting my recording app do the work of absorbing what he says. By the time he's finished, all the other customers have left and Martin is cleaning the tables, winding down for closing time.

'Thank you for your time, Mr Cooney,' I say, packing up my laptop. 'Your interview will be published in the next issue of the *Stakesville Chronicle*.' I force a smile that physically hurts.

'And thank you, Callum,' Tim Cooney says, shaking my hand once more. 'It was a pleasure talking to you. All the best for your studies.'

He toddles off, leaving me and Martin alone in the café.

'Wanker,' I mutter.

'Exactly what I was thinking,' Martin says.

ZELLE

My second day in Nicky's Knick Knacks goes exactly like the first.

By Wednesday, it already feels like I'm settled into a routine. Amazingly, I still haven't run into anyone I know: I'm straight in and out of the store, thanks to Mum dropping me off and picking me up. I bring food to work instead of buying it at the Four Square, and spend my break sitting outside the back of the building. Most of Nicky's customers are either tourists driving through the town or veteran collectors travelling here to pick up an item only she can offer. Basically, I'm able to relax. The past can't reach me here.

Until it does.

On Thursday, I'm trying to unjam the roll of receipt paper from the back of Nicky's ancient EFTPOS machine — third time it's got stuck this week — when I hear the doorbell. I'm too invested in trying to get this pathetic excuse for technology working again to bother looking up at who's come in. Besides, Nicky's already out on the shop floor, and it's not like customer service is something I'm itching to do. I keep my head down, focused on my task.

'Afternoon, Diana,' Nicky sings out.

I don't dare lift my head; hold onto the EFTPOS machine so tightly my knuckles throb. Keep my eyes down, hoping, hoping, hoping that it isn't—

'Hi, Nicky,' a woman replies, and I almost sob.

Because it's *her*.

The last person I want to see. One of the last people, at least.

I make a beeline for the back room.

Callum's mum is here to pick up the framed Grahame Sydney print I've seen lurking in the art section — for her office, she says. Diana Rig, MSc, PGDipClinPsych, PhD, one of the only clinical psychologists in a hundred-kilometre radius, *Ida Valley Moon* on the wall as she fixes Stakesville's mental health. She and Nicky make easy chit-chat as they lug the painting to the counter: Diana's recent office upgrades, debating on paint colours, the incoming warmer weather.

I'm completely out of sight here in the back room, but that doesn't stop the pounding of my heart and the cold sweat I feel on my spine. Truth is, Diana Rig is one of the loveliest people I know — a safe haven when Mum and Dad started fighting all the time. Something about her made me feel like I was always welcome, always wanted, always appreciated. God knows what she must think of me now.

I hear the ruffling of papers on the counter, Nicky's confused *hmmm*. 'Sorry,' she mutters, at the exact same moment I realise what it is that's gone missing: the EFTPOS machine I'm still holding on to for dear life. I know what's coming next.

'Zelle?' Nicky calls.

Cover blown.

Game over.

I keep my eyes fixed on the ground as I walk from the back room to the shop floor. Not that there's any point — it's not like there are many Zelles in the world to start with, certainly not in Central Otago.

'Sorry,' I mumble, not lifting my eyes, heaving the machine onto the counter. 'Receipt paper got jammed.'

Even without looking up, I can sense the moment Diana clocks that it's me. There's a stillness in the air, the smallest of gasps, and for the fleeting second I allow myself to look, I notice how Diana's eyes — hazel, just like Callum's — are wide with alarm, disbelief, surprise . . . and, along with the slight twitch of her mouth, what looks like sadness.

I know I should say something. There's no mistaken identity here, no doubt as to whether she's seeing who she thinks it is.

I run straight for the back room.

Even out of sight again I still feel exposed. I hide my face in my hands and fight the urge to cry. So, Callum *is* still here. He just didn't want to talk to me.

I don't blame him.

'Sorry about that,' Nicky says to Diana, and I don't know if she's apologising for the rogue EFTPOS machine, my running away, or both. They carry on as normal while Nicky finalises the payment, but I can practically feel the awkwardness between them, thick in the air like syrup. Graciously, though, Nicky doesn't mention why I'm here, and Diana doesn't ask.

But as soon as Diana leaves, Nicky's straight on my case.

'What was that all about?' she says, coming into the back room. 'You can't be running away from customers like that.' She shakes her head. 'That was Diana, too. Callum's mum.'

'Exactly,' I say, my teeth gritted.

Nicky studies me while I run my hands through my hair, trying to compose myself. 'Well, Callum was your best friend, wasn't he?' she says, and for the first time ever she doesn't sound sure of herself.

'Yeah,' I say. '*Was*.' I know I'm not making anything clearer. But I don't want to.

I wait for Nicky to figure it out. 'When's the last time you talked to Callum? And Diana?'

I look down, biting the inside of my cheek. 'Not since I left.'

'*Zelle*,' she sighs.

'What?'

'You know.' Nicky shakes her head slowly. 'It was a sad time, that summer you left. A sad time for the whole town.'

'I know that,' I say. 'I don't need you to remind me.'

We stare at each other for a long time. Finally, Nicky concedes.

'There's new stock to unpack,' she says. 'If you wouldn't mind.'

'Of course,' I say, and wander back to the shop floor.

I try to play a few riffs on my guitar that night, but I can't focus. Too many memories: of Fox and Mac, of Callum, of Eli. Memories of my dad.

My parents were never really happy together, not like most married couples should be, but the September before we moved out of Stakesville is when my parents went from *tolerating* to *hating* each other. That's when their usual petty arguments exploded into full-on fights.

One day in October:

Me, sitting in my room. Mum and Dad, arguing in the kitchen, not an unusual occurrence anymore. Voices mostly too muffled to really hear anything. Then:

Dad, really loud: That's ridiculous.

Mum: I don't believe you.

Dad: You're paranoid. Delusional.

Mum: Don't gaslight me, Walter.

Silence.

Mum: Give me your phone.

Dad: What?

Mum: Give it. Prove it to me. Prove to me that I'm paranoid.

Dad: No.

Mum: Look who's being ridiculous now.

Dad: Oh, fuck you.

And then something smashed: the kintsugi vase my parents had been gifted after their joint art exhibition opened in Tokyo. I don't know who threw it. I never asked. But it made a sound like the earth shattering, and in that moment I knew my own world had shattered too.

Mum came into my room later that night and apologised for the yelling. She said that she and Walter — she never referred to him as *Dad*, even when I was little — were going through a 'rough patch', that they were both stressed, that they were working through it. She didn't say what that fight was about, and I was too scared to ask. Plus, I had the sense that Mum would've lied about it if I did. But after that fight, things *did* get quieter. Only because Mum and Dad started sleeping in separate rooms. Only because their solution to not fighting was to barely talk to each other at all.

The best way to distract myself from the blur of memories is to call Luka. He doesn't know anything about my old life, and that makes him feel like my refuge more than ever. He answers on the third ring.

'Hey,' I say.

I can tell, immediately, that he must be out. There's so much noise: music, chatter, laughter. The sip of a drink. It feels like a kick in the chest.

'Hey. What's up?' Luka drawls.

'Are you in town?' I ask. It sounds like an accusation.

Luka laughs. 'Yes, Mother, I am in town. It's student

night, remember? Or have you turned into a country bumpkin already?'

Wednesday: the night when most of the bars in Wellington have their student deals. How could I forget?

'Of course,' I say.

'The others are here, too,' Luka says, practically speaking over the top of me. Then he's pulling the phone away from his mouth and yelling, 'It's Zelle!'

'Hi, Zelle!' I recognise the voices of Tabitha, Lucy and Anahera. Giggly with alcohol and excitement and *fun*.

I've never felt so hollow.

'Hey,' I say, aware that I'm most likely on speaker.

'Zelle!' Anahera screams down the line. 'How are you? How's your job? What did you say it was again? A thrift store?'

'Something like that,' I say. 'And, yeah, it's good. I'm good.'

'Yay! I'm so glad!'

In the background, Tabitha is shouting something about tequila shots.

'Sorry, hon,' Anahera says. 'Gotta go. Miss you, babes.'

'You, too,' I say, but she's already gone.

'Sorry about that,' Luka says. 'The bar's doing five-dollar tequila shots.'

'Well, I'd better leave you to it, then.' Suddenly I'm desperate to get off the call. I don't want to be reminded of everything I'm missing out on — of what my life used to be. 'Have fun.'

'You too!' Luka slurs. Then adds, laughing, 'If it's

possible down there.'

He hangs up.

I stare at the ceiling of my old bedroom, wondering how it's possible to come away from a conversation feeling even worse than I did before.

The house is eerily quiet. Our Wellington apartment was never silent: always there was the whir of traffic and wind and *life*. Always something to do, somewhere to be.

I've never felt so alone.

I close my eyes, leaving my guitar resting on my thighs. Snippets of the encounter with Diana play out like a movie. Dramatic silence as our eyes meet. Close-up on Diana's weary expression. Close-up on mine. Mid-shot of my turning body as I run for the back room. And then the camera poised on Diana and what I imagine would have been her look of bewilderment, confusion, disbelief.

And then I'm imagining Diana returning to her house, bursting into Callum's room and announcing *Zelle Bachmann's back*. Cal's look of terror, especially if he never received my text message. I'll see him again, inevitably. Probably at school. But how can I walk in there next Monday, in this place that's now so foreign, as if things can pick up from where they were left that easily?

I have to see him.

Talk to him.

Right now.

Before I can even think about what I'm doing, I put my guitar back in its case and grab my coat from my wardrobe. I lace up my Docs and creep out of my room and down the hallway. The door to Mum's room is closed, light spilling through the cracks, Kate Bush blasting on the stereo, but I don't dare make a sound, knowing she'll lose her shit if she hears me. It's not like there's anywhere I can really *go*, but Mum's treating me as if I'm under house arrest.

I open and close the back door as quietly as possible – a skill I've mastered over the last few years. Outside, it's darker and colder than I'd expected. I've forgotten how much harsher the weather is out here, balmy days followed by freezing cold nights. My breath puffs out small clouds of steam. The tips of my ears and nose itch.

I begin to jog down the driveway, headed straight for Callum's house.

CALLUM

After my interview with Tim Cooney I don't go straight home. Instead, I head to the local library and transcribe the interview, tucking myself away amongst the shelves of the non-fiction section. Cooney's homophobic tirade runs loops in my head. If only I had that on record.

Creating a new Word document, I title it *Tim Cooney,* and that's as far as I get before I'm staring at the blank page with the kind of existential dread that writers know best. Usually, as soon as I've finished and transcribed an interview, I'm ready to start drafting the feature: phrases and sentences come into my head fully formed, discovered rather than crafted.

Right now, though, I have nothing.

I make a start by writing down our unrecorded exchange:

TC: Never much liked that guy, to be honest.

CR: Why's that?

TC: Oh, you know. Very camp, isn't he?

CR: You don't like that?

TC: People should have the freedom to do as they please, but there's no need to . . . you know. Show off about it. Stick it in everyone's faces.

CR: He's just being himself, isn't he?

TC: Hm. Is he?

I save the document and call it a day.

When I get back, Mum and Kate are already started on eating dinner. Descartes, hopeful for scraps, sits by their feet.

'Hi, love,' Mum says. She sounds as chirpy as ever, but she looks tired. 'How was Tim Cooney?'

'All right,' I say, flinging myself into the seat opposite her and Kate, eyeing the plate of food waiting for me. I shove a forkful of pasta in my mouth to avoid any more discussion of Tim Cooney.

'So, who was the boy by the gate this morning?' Mum asks.

'His name's Finn,' I say.

'Where's he from?'

'Alex.'

'What's he doing in Stakesville?'

'His dad's a doctor, apparently. Working at the medical centre.'

'He'll be Dr Ranjani's replacement,' Mum says. Small-town knowledge. 'So, is Finn your friend?'

'I've known him for less than forty-eight hours, so

slightly too early to say, I think.'

'It would be nice for you to make a new friend,' Mum says. What she really means is: it would be nice for you to make a new *best* friend. Because, since Zelle, I haven't had a friend as tight as we were. Not even close.

Mum takes a deep breath. She sighs. Taps her fingertips along the tabletop like she's preparing something to say.

Then she says it.

'I think I saw Zelle Bachmann today.'

I freeze. Kate chokes on her water.

'*What*?' she splutters.

It takes me a moment to catch my breath, to not be completely consumed by panic. 'Where?'

'At Nicky's store,' Mum says. 'I was there to pick up a painting, and I saw Zelle working out the back . . . it must have been her. Had to be.'

'She's back?' Kate squawks. 'Why the hell is she back?'

Mum studies me. Her face is calm, as always, but I see a glimmer of sadness in her eyes. We barely ever talk about Zelle. Zelle's name is one we always skirt around, politely ignore, the big looming elephant in the room that we always pretend isn't there. It's taboo. Completely off-limits.

'Have you heard anything from her?' Mum asks.

There's no use in trying to hide anything now: I nod.

'*Cal!*' Kate shouts. 'Why didn't you say anything before?'

'Because I didn't want *this* to happen,' I say, suddenly angry, using my fork to gesture to the drama unfolding between us. I hate making a scene. Especially if it involves Zelle. Especially if it involves talking about what happened the summer we turned fourteen.

'*This*,' Kate says, stabbing the air with her own fork, 'isn't just any old friend coming back from the past. This is Zelle Bachmann, Callum. Your best friend. Your best friend who screwed you over.'

Kate has Very Strong Feelings about what happened with Zelle.

'Kate,' Mum warns.

'It's true!'

'Do you ever shut up?' I say.

'Callum,' Mum snaps.

'You know it's more complicated than that,' I say, feeling like a deflated balloon.

'Well, it's not complicated to *me*,' Kate retorts, her eyes vicious. 'She ruined you, Callum. She left you in the dust. There's only one way to feel about that.'

'Don't tell me how to feel about it, Kate.'

We glower at each other.

'I have to,' she says. 'Because you won't.'

'Hey,' Mum says as I get up from my chair. 'I know it's not easy to talk about, but this is a big deal.'

'Of course I fucking know it's a big deal,' I snap.

She doesn't even tell me off for cursing.

'Come on, Callum. At least let's discuss this properly.'

'There's nothing to discuss,' I say as I kick my chair in, stomp down the hallway and shut my bedroom door with a satisfying slam.

Of course Mum knocks on my door a couple of hours later. Kate hasn't come anywhere near me: she's too stubborn to say sorry in the immediate aftermath of an argument.

'Can I come in?' Mum asks, her voice muffled through the door.

I give a grunt of approval, though it's not like I can say no anyway.

I'm lying on my bed, looking through the gallery in my phone camera marked *Eli*. It's not just photos of him; it's photos of all of us from our first year of high school, from our last summer together as the Famous Five. I find my gaze stuck on photos of Zelle, her blue eyes glimmering, her smile always dialled up to the max. Always brighter, always just *more* than anyone else.

Mum sits down at the edge of the bed. 'I think it would be good to talk about Zelle.'

I arch an eyebrow. 'If I wanted to do that, I'd pay two hundred dollars to book an appointment with you.'

She smirks. 'I'm saying this as your mother, not your therapist.'

'Well, coincidentally you happen to be both.'

'Consider it a bonus,' Mum says. She peers over my shoulder to see what's on my phone, and I don't quite manage to turn the screen off in time.

'Is that Eli?'

I sit up, drawing my knees to my chest. 'Yeah.'

And this is where I once again appreciate my mother and her PhD-level expertise in Talking About Hard Things, because she lets us sit in the silence together, doesn't cajole me for answers for things I don't want to say, doesn't feel the need to state the obvious. All she does is shift across the bed until she's sitting right next to me and I feel comfortable enough to rest my head on her shoulder.

'Have you talked to Fox and Mac about this?'

I shake my head.

She doesn't get mad.

'Well, maybe you should,' she says mildly.

'Maybe,' I say, even though I know an uncomfortable conversation with them is inevitable. It's not like I can live in denial about Zelle's reappearance now.

Which gets me thinking.

Panicking, more like.

Zelle is back. Has *moved* back. Already landed a job at Nicky's Knick Knacks. And more likely than not is coming back to school. Can I wait that long to see her? Have her appear in the classroom and straight back into my life as if nothing's changed? Can I deal with that?

Even though Mum's confirmed the truth, there's a part of my brain that's still hoping all of this is a dream.

I have to see her.

Talk to her.

Right now.

'You all right, Cal?' Mum asks, noticing the hitch in my breath.

I lift my head off her shoulder. 'Yeah. Fine. Actually, I think I might go see Fox. And Mac. To talk.'

'Right now?'

I'm already pulling on my hoodie. 'I need to.'

'Are you sure that's a good idea?'

'I can't do it in class,' I say. 'And I don't want to hold off. In case Zelle comes back to school.'

That convinces her, though it doesn't ease the dent between her brows. 'Well, okay. Don't be out too late, though. And stay safe.'

As if there are pick-pocketers and thugs crawling Mistakesville's streets.

'Of course,' I say.

'Home by ten.'

'I'm not on my restricted licence anymore.'

'Home by ten, Callum. You've got school tomorrow.'

It's nearly nine-thirty already.

'Fine. Roger that, Captain,' I say.

'See you tonight, Private.' Mum smiles, salutes, and finally leaves me to it.

I spend a few minutes just standing there before hurrying to the front door where Mum's left the car keys on the hook of the coat rack. I put on my shoes, call out a 'See ya!' and close the door behind me. I unlock the car. Put the key in the ignition.

And before I can think too deeply about it, I start the engine and begin the drive to The Sanctuary.

ZELLE

It's almost unbearably cold outside, but at least it gives me something to focus on. I start to feel a little calmer.

Before I know it, I'm all the way down the driveway and onto the gravel road. And suddenly I'm sprinting, my breath filling the silence, the fire in my legs distracting me from the cold. Round the bend and our country road meets the main one, like a river meeting the ocean.

I don't bother to look before I dart across.

Can't hear anything beyond my thumping pulse and heavy breath.

Only notice the car when the horn blares, the brakes squeal, and I roll onto the bitumen before the car can beat me to it.

CALLUM

I'm almost at the turnoff to Zelle's road when something darts out in front of me.

At first I think it's an animal — a sheep or a goat, or a deer, maybe. But in the tenth of a second it takes for me to register the movement, I realise it's not an animal at all.

It's a person.

And they haven't noticed me.

My body takes charge over my brain. I slam on the brakes and blare the horn, feel the car shuddering like a jet plane landing in turbulence. Finally, *finally,* the person notices, eyes wide with panic, far too late.

I grind to a halt just as they hit the ground.

ZELLE

My hands are raw with tar and gravel. My knees sting like they've been stripped to the bone.

There's the sound of a car door slamming, footsteps running towards me. I stay on the ground, frozen on all fours, unwilling to move, unwilling to make it real.

'Oh, fuck. Fuck. Fuck. Fuck,' a voice stammers. A voice that snaps me out of my shocked state.

A voice that I recognise.

I turn my head. Roll onto my butt.

And fuck me sideways.

It's him.

CALLUM

I've just hit someone with my car.

My hands shake so badly it's almost impossible to get the key out of the ignition. I want to throw up. But I fight the urge, turn on the car's hazard lights and run towards the figure on the road.

'Oh, fuck,' I say. 'Fuck. Fuck. Fuck.'

The person rolls over. A girl. Wild-eyed and ghostly pale.

And oh shit.

It's her.

ZELLE

It's Callum.

CALLUM

It's Zelle.

ZELLE

Oh, God.

CALLUM

I'm going to be sick.

ZELLE

The first thing Cal does is throw up.

Right in the middle of the road.

It's a comically Cal-like gesture. But now's not really the time to say so.

He wipes his hand across his mouth and looks up.

'Oh my God,' he says. 'Oh my God. Fuck. I'm so sorry. I'm so sorry. Oh, God—'

'I'm fine,' I say, seeing the way he's shaking, how he looks like he's on the edge of bawling. 'You didn't hit me. I'm fine. I rolled out of the way.'

He looks down at my scraped-up palms.

'You're bleeding.'

'It's minor. Just grazes. Barely hurts.' Actually, it hurts like hell, but there's no point saying that.

'Fuck,' he says again, and closes his eyes. I know he's having a Classic Cal Freak Out — I've seen many of them —

but he's obviously forgotten that we're right in the middle of a dark, remote, potholed South Island highway, two sitting ducks for any car careening through at a hundred kilometres an hour.

'Not to spoil the mood,' I say. 'But you should probably move your car.'

Callum snaps his eyes open like he's been woken from a deep sleep, like he's been planted into a different universe. Then, mechanically, he gets to his feet. For a moment I don't know what to do, then I realise I should probably follow him. I ease myself up from the ground, biting down the urge to swear as I straighten up. When I look down, there are two dark patches blooming on the knees of my jeans.

Cal opens the driver's door and clambers in; tentatively, I slide into the passenger seat. It's weird seeing Cal in the driver's seat: it feels like we're still fourteen, waiting in the car for our parents and sitting in the front for fun. Kids pretending to be adults.

Cal starts the ignition and eases us into the safety of the road shoulder, a grassy verge banking tall pine trees. He turns off the engine and kills the headlights. The only light is from the stars. We're silent for so long, it feels like the whole world has gone quiet.

'When'd you dye your hair?' Callum asks finally, just as I'm searching for something to say.

'Oh. Um.' I pick up a lock and twirl it between my fingers. 'In January, I think.' And since we're on the topic of appearances, and I can think of nothing else to say,

I add, 'You're so much taller than the last time I saw you.'

He doesn't respond, which is fair, because I guess there's really nothing you can say to that. But still. He's not helping me out here.

'What were you doing running down the highway?' he bursts out at last. The shock and fear are still fresh on his face. 'I was so scared. I thought I'd hit you.'

I run my fingers over the grazed knuckles of my other hand, the blood already drying and sticky. I suppress a wince. 'I was going to yours,' I admit, realising that lying would be futile. 'Where were *you* going?'

'To yours,' Cal says.

We lock eyes.

'I texted you,' I say.

'I know.'

'Why'd you drive here then?'

Cal closes his eyes, exhales through his nose. 'My mum said she saw you at Nicky's today.'

It's not really an explanation, so I press on. 'Well, you could've replied to my text.'

Callum flutters his eyes open. 'I wasn't sure it was real,' he says. 'I thought maybe you were lying.'

'I wouldn't lie about something like that, Cal,' I say, offended, even though I have no right to be. 'I wouldn't lie to you.'

He glares at me as I say that, and I know what we're both thinking: that statement is a lie, too.

'Why are you here, Zelle?' he says. 'Why'd you come back?'

And it feels like salt straight onto my grazes to lie to him again, but I can't afford to tell the truth. 'Mum's refurbishing The Sanctuary,' I tell him. 'It needed to be done. We'll probably put it on the market once it's been renovated. And, also, you know, we left here pretty hastily. It was about time we came back and tidied things up. Metaphorically *and* literally. What about you?' I say, desperate to change the subject. 'How's your mum? And Kate?'

'Good. Fine.'

'And Descartes?'

'Still going,' he says, the smallest of smiles playing at his lips.

'Oh, thank God,' I say, genuinely relieved. 'Nicky told me about Biscuit.'

Cal frowns. 'Yeah. That was a while ago now.'

'And Fox and Mac? They're still here?'

'Yep.'

'Still friends?'

'Of course.'

I swallow. 'What about the Gibsons?'

I can't say Eli's name. Not now. Not yet. Asking whether his family's still here is the closest I can get to acknowledging his presence.

A beat passes. Two beats. Four. 'They moved to Christchurch,' he says finally. 'Six months after you left.'

'Oh,' I say. 'I didn't know.'

'You wouldn't.'

'Callum.'

His gaze is fixed out the window.

'I'm sorry,' I say.

He whips around, suddenly fierce. 'You should've said that three years ago.'

I fight the lump that grows thick in my throat. 'I—'

I jump as Cal's phone starts ringing, the blare like whiplash.

'Sorry,' he says, grabbing his phone from his pocket, holding it to his ear. 'Hi. Yeah. Sorry. I'm fine. Just lost track of time. I'm sorry. I'll come home now. See you soon.'

He rubs his hand along his forehead. 'I have to go,' he tells me.

I don't know how to answer.

I don't want to stay. But I don't want to leave.

'I'll drive you back,' he says.

'You don't have to.'

'You're hurt. And it's safer,' he says.

I should be grateful, but I hate how cold he sounds. He drives off without another word. This time I don't scramble to make conversation, because I know there's nothing I can say. Without me having to ask, Cal slows down a good few paces before the lip of the hill, stopping the car before we're fully in sight of The Sanctuary.

'Thank you,' I say. 'And I'm sorry for what happened tonight.'

He shrugs.

I click off my seatbelt.

'I'll see you at school, I guess. I start on Monday.'

Another shrug.

'Will we talk, Cal?'

He shakes his head. 'I don't know, Zelle,' he sighs. 'I really don't.'

He doesn't drive away until I'm safely over the rise of the hill and down the other side. The sound of the engine fades into the still night like steam and disappears completely as I slink in through the back door. The house is quiet. I sneak into the bathroom and wash the grit from my grazes.

I don't let myself cry until I've closed my bedroom door.

CALLUM

'I told you to be home by ten,' Mum calls from the lounge as I come in the door. 'I was getting worried.'

'I'm sorry,' I say. My eyes feel glassy and my voice is wobbling, so I take my time unlacing my shoes until I can keep the quiver in my throat under control.

'How did it go?' she asks.

I stand up, shaking the ache out of my shoulders. 'I don't really want to talk about it,' I say.

As I walk down the hallway to my bedroom, Kate is lingering in the doorway of her own room, hovering like a ghost. I hadn't noticed her at first, which means I haven't had the chance to hide the tears pooling in my eyes before she sees. But she just *knows*, in her Kate way, and wordlessly tackles me into a bear hug that reminds me why she is, despite everything, my favourite person in the world.

'Sorry I'm a bitch,' she says.

'Apology accepted.'

I escape to my room and crash onto my bed, closing my eyes against the glare of the light. Eventually I fall into a fitful half-sleep, still fully dressed, still on top of the covers.

The familiar scratch of claws on carpet wakes me. I get up and open the door, and Descartes mews a hello before brushing past my legs and swaggering in.

I help him up onto the bed, and he doesn't even scratch me while I cry into his fur.

The next morning is the unavoidable talk. Not just with Mum, but with my friends.

I wish I really had gone to see Fox and Mac last night, broken the news to them in private. It will have to be on the walk to school: not ideal, though private enough to have the inevitable freak-out in peace.

But there's a problem.

The Finn problem.

Knowing him, he'll be waiting outside my house, just like yesterday.

The only solution is to set my alarm to get up fifteen minutes earlier than usual and race to get ready.

'You're up early,' Mum remarks. She's not yet in her frantic scramble to get to work (that's how early it is).

I shrug. 'Got lots to do today. Assignments. Tim Cooney article.'

'Are you meeting Finn before school?'

I give her the side eye. 'Maybe,' I say.

'Do you want to tell me how it went last night?'

I take a deep breath. 'Okay, I think. Not great. But we'll deal with it.'

I can only hope that's true.

I manage to leave the house early enough to avoid Finn, but jog to my usual meeting point with Fox and Mac just to be sure.

Fox arrives first. He waves to me across the street, running to catch up.

'Mac's a couple of minutes behind. She forgot her phone. You're early,' he adds. Predictably.

'Thought I'd change it up,' I say. I try to seem relaxed so that I can wait until Mac gets here before I make my big announcement. Unfortunately, I am not a very good actor. And, unfortunately, Fox is very good at reading my expressions.

'What's up?' he says.

I feign confusion. 'What do you mean, what's up?'

He rolls his eyes. 'You're full of shit, Cal. Something's wrong.'

'I—' Everything I'd rehearsed has exited my brain like fog through a window. 'Can we wait until Mac gets here?'

His expression softens. 'Is it bad?'

'I'd rather talk about it with Mac here too.'

'Did you not get into broadcasting school?'

(Talk about rubbing salt into the wound.) 'I don't hear back for weeks, Fox.'

'Okay. Good. Good it's not that, at least.'

'Hey!' Mac, perpetually cheery, charges across the road

to join us. She instantly clocks our glum expressions. 'Is everything all right?' she says.

Fox nudges me. 'Cal?'

Even with hundreds of rehearsals, a million run-throughs of the scenario in my mind, my stupid anxious brain is never prepared for the real thing. 'I . . . um . . . I got a text last week. From Zelle.'

The quiet that follows is like thunderclouds over a broad blue sky. Fox and Mac's faces go flat, lips pressed into thin lines. Thing is, we've never really discussed Zelle. That summer happened, Zelle and Eli disappeared, and we moved on. Zelle's not so much a person in our lives as a figment of our imaginations, a distant memory, a half-formed thought. Here, saying her name out loud, bringing her into the present, is like bringing her back to life.

'What did she want?' Mac says. Her voice is cold.

'She. Well.' I swallow. 'She told me she's coming back to Mistakesville. Well, actually, that she *is* back—'

Mac holds out a hand to stop me. 'What do you mean, *back*?' she says, and if the silence before felt like thunderclouds, then Mac's voice is the storm: angry, vicious, brooding. 'As in, visiting?'

I see the hope light up in her and Fox's faces. I can't look them in the eyes as I say, 'Well. Um. No.'

'What do you mean, no?' both of them say.

'You mean that she's *moved* back?' Mac continues. 'Like, permanently?'

And that's when we hear another 'Hey!' bounce across the street.

Our heads snap up. Walking towards us, bag slung over one shoulder, lazy grin plastered to his face, is Finn.

Oh, God.

Not now.

'Hey,' he says again. He's crossed the road and is only a few metres from us. 'You outran me, Callum.' If he's peeved that I left without him, he doesn't show it. Not that we ever established that walking to school together was going to be a thing we did.

'Sorry,' I say.

'Zelle's *moved* back, Callum?' Mac isn't going to let this go.

I glance at Finn, now standing on the fringe of our group looking thoroughly confused. I tilt my head towards him as subtly as I can. 'Maybe we shouldn't talk about this right now—'

'What the hell do you know about Zelle Bachmann?' Mac barks.

Okay, then. I guess we are talking about it now.

With an audience.

'She's here with her mum, apparently. Renovating The Sanctuary. I saw her last night.' Fox and Mac don't respond, so I babble on. 'I would've told you about the text earlier, but I wasn't sure what to believe, and I didn't want to bring it up and cause a fuss in case she was lying or nothing came out of it, then yesterday my mum said she saw her working in Nicky's Knick Knacks, and so I felt like I had to see her for myself, to make it real, I don't know, and so I drove up to The Sanctuary last night and she was right there on the road, walking to my house – actually, I almost hit her with my car . . . and, anyway. We talked. And she's here. And she's coming back to school next week.'

At last I realise that no amount of rambling is going to snap Fox and Mac out of their stunned silence, or make the situation seem any less bad than it is.

(Finn, thankfully, has the good grace not to say anything.)

It feels like a lifetime passes before Fox comes up with the perfect response.

'This is kind of shit, isn't it?' he says.

Mac stares off, wistful, then squeezes her eyes shut. 'We're so close to the end of the year,' she says.

I know what she means. It's August now: only a couple more months of school, then exams, and then we're done with school forever. And then we're off to university, leaving Mistakesville behind for good, and Zelle will never be able to meddle with our lives again. We were so close to escaping her. Escaping her and Eli and that terrible summer.

But we don't have that freedom anymore.

'What do we do?' Fox says.

We exchange looks. All of us shrug.

'I don't know,' I say. 'I really don't.'

It's then that we realise that no amount of dawdling is going to make the situation any less awkward. In silent agreement we unstick ourselves from the pavement and head down the street in single file. Mac first, so far ahead that you couldn't talk to her if you tried. Fox next, his shoulders slumped, radiating the message that he wants to be left alone. And behind me, trailing us like a lost puppy, is Finn.

'I know I probably wasn't supposed to hear that,' he says to me. 'But who's Zelle?'

'My best friend,' I say. '*Old* best friend.'

'Did shit happen?'

Did shit happen.

I look up at the sky: the hints of sun that were there when I left the house have been shrouded by tired, grey clouds. Fitting.

'It's a bit more complicated than that,' I say.

Stakesville's Main Man: An Interview with Tim Cooney (first draft)

By Callum Rig

Councillor Tim Cooney has represented the Stakesville ward on the Central Otago Regional Council for the past three years. And now, with the local body elections coming up, he's hoping to serve for three more. Here Tim Cooney discusses his achievements, goals and vision for the Stakesville area.

Tim Cooney is passionate about this corner of the world. When we meet in Perfect Mistakes café—

If there's one thing to know about councillor Tim Cooney, it's that he lives, breathes and loves this corner of the world—

One thing's for sure about Tim Cooney: it's that he's—

Tim Cooney has—

Tim Cooney is—

fuck it

[Document saved]

ZELLE

It's Monday.

It's back to school.

I get ready so slowly you'd think my body was made of lead. I drag myself out of bed, drag myself into the shower, drag myself into light-blue jeans and my Basquiat tee-shirt, drag mascara through my eyelashes and foundation on my cheeks, drag myself to the kitchen to drag a coffee from our espresso machine. Mum snaps at me for being so slow, but I genuinely can't help it. Even if I wasn't stalling for time, I couldn't go any faster.

I'm dragging my toothbrush across my teeth when Mum loses it.

'I told you to be ready five minutes ago,' she snaps.

I try to talk with the foam in my mouth. 'Two more minutes.'

'Zelle!'

'That's what the dentists tell you—'

Mum storms down the hallway.

I spit into the sink.

'Where are you going?' I yell.

'To the car,' she shouts back. 'If you're not out by 8.15 I'm coming inside to drag you out.'

It's 8.14.

I practically run after her, grabbing my backpack and shoes from the doorway. Mum's already started the car.

'Hurry!' she shouts.

I fling open the passenger door. 'My shoes aren't even on!'

'Put them on in the car!'

'Give it a rest! You're so *infuriating*.'

'Well, you're not helping,' Mum retorts.

'Well, neither are you,' I say.

Mum doesn't reply. Probably because she knows it's true.

We drive the rest of the way to school in silence. The nearer we get, the further I sink in my seat while still trying to peek out to see if Cal, Fox and Mac are around.

'Can you drop me off here?' I say when we're still a couple of hundred metres away. I can see the school buildings now, the footpath filling up with students. I want to be inconspicuous. Defer my last minutes of anonymity for a little longer.

'I'll drop you off by the gates,' Mum replies. Translation via the firmness of her voice: she doesn't trust me not to skive off.

I sigh.

Mum slows down by the crowded main entrance.

I'm a sardine in a pool of sharks.

'Remember to go to Mr Banks's office first,' Mum says. 'He'll give you your timetable.'

I unclip my seatbelt and don't say anything. Grab my bag by the strap and place my other hand on the door handle.

'I'll pick you up after school.'

I swing open the door.

'Be good, Zelle,' Mum says, which stops me dead.

I turn my head to look at her. There's something in her eyes I don't recognise, and something in her voice I don't recognise either.

'I'll see you after school,' I say, and even my own voice sounds foreign to me.

'Welcome back, Giselle Bachmann,' Mr Banks says. His smile is like Jabba the Hutt's. 'Long time, no see, isn't it? A very long time indeed.'

I don't answer. I'd almost forgotten how our principal speaks like a Shakespearean actor. I wait for him to get to the point.

He coughs awkwardly. 'Right-o. I've got your timetable printed out here. You've got maths with Mr Abassi first.' He points at the page as if I don't know how to read. 'You remember Mr Abassi, don't you?'

'Does a bear shit in the woods?' I mumble. Mr Abassi is the *only* senior maths teacher at Stakesville Area School.

He's been here since the gold rush started, or thereabouts.

'Come on, Giselle,' Mr Banks says. 'That's not the kind of attitude we tolerate here.' He nods towards the poster behind his desk that proclaims *SCHOOL VALUES: Success, respect, care and progress!* Written beneath is our school motto: *Mining the best of everyone since 1862.*

Honestly.

Mr Banks waves my timetable at me. 'Okey-dokey, Giselle, you'd best be off to class. Good luck on your first day, and remember to bring the right attitude,' he says, as if my *right attitude* is a sandwich in the lunchbox deep down in the bottom of my schoolbag.

'Thank you,' I mumble, because I know I owe him a little bit of decency.

Mr Banks smiles his slimy Jabba smile, and I practically run out the door. I remember the way to Mr Abassi's classroom and, given that this school's about a fifth of the size as my old school in Wellington, it's not exactly hard to regain my bearings. I make it in less than two minutes. My heart is thundering.

I swing open the door.

And I'm swallowed whole.

CALLUM

It's the day Zelle first moved to Mistakesville all over again.

I'm sitting with Fox and Mac and Finn in maths and we're acting like it's just a normal day, even though there's a gnawing at my stomach because today is *the* day and none of us says so because maybe not saying anything means it isn't real.

And maybe because nothing can prepare you for the moment it happens.

I'm busy looking down at my notebook when the door creaks open and Mr Abassi claps his hands and says, 'Class,' and everything stops and everybody goes quiet and Mac and Fox go rigid, and half the class gasps because it's her and she's right there and it's *real*.

And I am nine years old and sitting at my desk before school starts and the strange new girl walks in with her strange parents and her owl-wide eyes scan the classroom and lock on me and she bounces over with her strange accent and her hands clasping a steelblue ladybird and she lets me in on her secret and she chooses me and I feel like the most important person in the world.

And right now it's all the same, and Zelle is standing at the front of the class with her owl-wide eyes that lock on mine, but instead of being open and friendly and curious she looks the most afraid I've ever seen her.

ZELLE

'Exciting times for us,' Mr Abassi announces to the class. 'We've got a second new student in the space of a week. This person will be familiar to most of you, though. Zelle, welcome back to Stakesville.'

And my eyes find Cal's in the crowd almost immediately, and instead of the anchor they felt like on my first day of school, they cast me adrift even more.

Mr Abassi tells me to take a seat.

'Go on, Zelle,' he nudges, when I've been frozen for too long. 'The joys of mathematics await.'

My cheeks are flaming.

I can feel the classroom's collective shock.

I want to run away.

Unfortunately, taking a seat means having to look up to find one. I lift my head slowly, and it's like I'm a celebrity amid a swarm of paparazzi — eyes wide, mouths agape, an electric buzz in the air signalling that for once something interesting is happening. Christ, I recognise almost everyone here. There's only a couple of unfamiliar faces, and a couple who aren't here anymore. And no Eli, of course.

My eyes drift to the back left corner.

There, looking the most panic-stricken of everyone, sitting in the same spot they always have, are Cal, Fox and Mac.

And a stranger.

My replacement, I think. Or Eli's replacement. But I immediately feel horrible for thinking that.

There's a spare seat at their table.

I can see Fox and Mac pleading with their eyes for me not to come sit with them. Callum's face is just a mask of horror so pure I can't tell what he's thinking. I hope he doesn't throw up, for his own sake and for everyone else's. This stranger guy sitting next to him looks less intimidated, but I can tell he's also standing in solidarity.

I'm taking too long.

I'm starting to panic.

Mr Abassi's getting impatient.

Everyone keeps staring at me.

I sit down at Callum's table.

'Let's begin,' Mr Abassi says, clapping his hands together in a way that makes me jump. Mac and Fox glare at me. Callum won't look at me. The stranger is on Callum's left side, so I can't see him. The way the seating's arranged, it's a pod of four, plus my desk at the end, making me head of the table. Or the outsider.

I'm not sure what I should do, so I raise my hand in a wave and whisper, 'Hi.'

Nobody responds.

The lesson goes on.

Mr Abassi teaches us how to do something with trigonometry that none of us are ever going to use, but I write down notes anyway, pressing my pencil so hard I tear a hole through the thin leaf of my notebook. I glance up to see the others pretending to be as engrossed in the lesson as I am, except for Cal, who's staring at me. As soon as he sees I've noticed, he looks away. After that I can't even pretend to concentrate, especially knowing that Cal's still sneaking looks at me every half second, so I put my pencil down and rub my temples. The increasing pounding in my head's worse than a hangover headache.

'Is trigonometry important?' Mr Abassi asks. He picks up his mug of coffee — it says *Maths puns are the first SINE of madness*, shoot me now — and sits down at his desk, suddenly so deep in thought it's as if he's having a crisis of career. He turns to our corner of the room. 'Finn. New to this town, not new to the area. What do you think? Is trigonometry of significance to your life?'

Finn. That's the stranger at our table. He clears his throat, seemingly at ease with being called out in class. 'Is this in my objective opinion or my subjective opinion?'

'Your opinion is your opinion, Mr Nassar.'

'Well—'

I see that Callum's full attention is now focused on Finn.

He pushes up his glasses and twitches his nose, something he does when he's feeling self-conscious.

'I'm sorry to say, sir, but I do struggle to see the relevance of trigonometry. In my own life, at least.'

'Wrong!' Mr Abassi bellows.

Finn looks at Mr Abassi like he's just told him to get out.

'But sir, you asked for his opinion,' Mac counters, ever the arguer. She's been on the school's debating team since Year Nine. 'You can't call an opinion wrong.'

'You can if they don't have the logic to support their argument, Mackenzie. That's the fundamental principle of philosophy.'

'This is Year Thirteen maths, sir.'

'Do you know what this is?' Mr Abassi interrupts, and dear God, he pulls out a *map*. He unfurls it and sticks it on the whiteboard.

'It's a map,' Mac says. Helpfully.

'A map of *what*?'

'The town,' Piper Kohrt says from the front.

Mr Abassi points at her. 'Top of the class.' Then he addresses all of us. 'Our very own town was founded on a trigonometry mistake. William Stakes, the gold miner and namesake of our town who surveyed this land, obviously didn't have me for a teacher, did he?'

Nobody laughs.

'As a group task,' Mr Abassi says, 'I want you all to go back to early 1860s New Zealand. You are pioneers freshly arrived to begin a new life on the plains of Central Otago—'

'Colonisers, you mean,' says Mac.

'And it is your task to use trigonometry to plot where our town should go,' continues Mr Abassi. 'Try not to make the same mistake as Mr Stakes. And bonus points for coming up with a new name for the town.'

Mr Abassi hands out photocopies of the map that's on the whiteboard and gives one to each table. Cal, Fox, Mac and Finn swarm to it like seagulls. So much for group work, then.

I want to scream at them how childish it is to pretend I'm not even there, but when I think about the wider circumstances I find my argument probably doesn't have the logic to support it. Philosophically speaking.

'Fuck.' Fox is frowning at his calculator. 'Is that right?'

Finn peers over at the map. 'Judging by your calculations, our town would be in the lake, so probably not.'

'Atlantisville,' Mac says.

They squabble over how to fix their calculations. One thing that hasn't changed about my old friends is that they're all God-awful at maths. And it appears that new-boy Finn is just as much of a lost cause as the rest of them.

'You're doing it wrong,' I say.

They all turn to me as if they didn't know I could speak.

'Pass me the calculator,' I ask Fox.

Reluctantly, he hands it over.

'See. This is how you do it.' I punch in the numbers. When I've got the answer, I reach over with my pencil and mark it on the map. Right where the real Stakesville was meant to be. 'Done. Now. Shall we name it?'

They gape at me like fish.

Mac blinks furiously, like she's woken up in a different universe. 'Um. Suppose in honour of this class we could call it Abassiville?'

Fox winces. 'That's just as bad as Stakesville.'

'Trigonometryville, then?'

'Does it have to end in *-ville*?'

'Can we stop pretending as if I'm not here?' I say.

Stunned faces once more.

Mac bites first. 'Because you answered a maths question for us doesn't make us friends again,' she snaps.

'Well, acting like I don't exist isn't going to make us friends either,' I say.

Mac glowers. 'You acted like we didn't exist for three whole years, so why can't we do the same to you?'

'Mac,' Fox warns.

Callum already has his hands over his face.

Finn scrawls something down on the sheet of paper and calls Mr Abassi over to check.

'I went with Abassiville,' he says. 'Hope you don't mind.'

CALLUM

After maths, I don't see Zelle for the rest of the day. I have media studies, then English, then I have a free period before history in the afternoon, which basically means I have a whole two-hour break in the middle of the day. I spend my study period in the library, trying to do more work on my Tim Cooney piece, but I can't write anything more under the measly standfirst I've already written, so I give up and read for the rest of the period. And try not to think about Tim Cooney, or Keri, or broadcasting school. Or Zelle.

At lunch, I go to meet the others at our patch of grass under the oak tree. I realise I'm half expecting Zelle to be with them. To my relief, she's not.

'No Zelle?' I ask Fox as I find a place to sit between him and Mac and opposite Finn.

'Nope. Haven't seen her since maths.'

'And thank God for that,' Mac pipes up. She's lying on her back with her arm over her eyes. 'Her voice does my head in. So does her hair.'

I tug out a patch of grass while Mac swiftly changes the subject and chatters to Finn about Joe Rooney's woolshed party on Friday night. Joe hosts his party every August, and it's one of the highlights of the year, given that it's basically the only time in Mistakesville when something actually *happens*. It's a tradition that's been going since Joe's oldest brother Jack began it when he was in high school, then Joe's middle brother Conan took over when *he* was in school, and now it's Joe's legacy to continue. Mistakesville will become even more boring once Joe graduates high school and leaves town.

'You'll love it,' Mac says to Finn. 'It's the only good thing that ever happens here.'

'That sets the bar pretty low,' Finn replies, but I can tell he's the type of person who'd enjoy himself no matter how shitty a party is, and while I'm looking at him he throws a smile my way and he has dimples deep enough to sail boats in.

Lethal.

Mac points at me. 'Even Cal enjoys it, and he's not usually a party person.'

'Last year he enjoyed Joe's sangria so much he threw up behind a silo,' Fox adds, and everyone laughs while I feel my cheeks flare.

'I didn't realise he'd put so much brandy in it,' I mumble, all too aware of Finn's eyes on me and doing my best not to look at him back.

'Poor Cal doesn't have a strong stomach,' Mac says. Completely unnecessarily. She drapes an arm around my shoulders, her voice light and mocking. 'It's his party trick.'

Fox grins wickedly. 'Remember that time when—'

'Please don't finish that sentence,' I say, my head in my hands. I'm feigning despair, but I really am mortified at my friends' pure evilness, how they know exactly what embarrasses me most, how they just *know*. I raise my head, and everyone's grinning at me maniacally, like I'm being stared down by three Cheshire cats.

Finn gets up and announces he's going to the bathroom. 'Don't tell any more embarrassing Cal stories without me,' he says. 'I'd hate to miss out.'

My cheeks go from flushed to full-on flames. Fox and Mac are still laughing, and I'm praying they don't notice how my face has caught fire. I wait until Finn's gone before I speak.

'Maybe we should invite Zelle to the party,' I say.

And that kills their laughter quick smart.

Mac quirks an eyebrow. 'You're fucking joking,' she says in a tone so serious it's not even a question, not even an option that's open for debate.

I swallow.

'Isn't she right, though?' I say.

'Right about what?' Fox says.

Mac says nothing.

'Well.' I look down, wondering if I've gone too far. If

I'm doing the right thing. 'She's here now, isn't she? And it's a little bit weird to just carry on as if she's not.'

'What are you suggesting, Callum?' Mac's voice is icy. 'A fucking friendship reunion? Throwing a welcome home party?'

'I just thought it would be . . . nice,' I gabble, wishing I hadn't said anything at all.

'You think we should talk to her,' Fox says. 'Let her talk to us.'

Goddamn him, knowing me too well. 'I mean—'

'No,' Mac says. 'What's there for her to say? She did the unforgivable. She wasn't there when we needed her. When *you* needed her. She wasn't there for Eli. Didn't even bother to talk to us after what happened. Just fucked off to live her ritzy life in Wellington without a single acknowledgement of us. Didn't even *tell* us she was leaving Stakesville. There's no coming back from that.'

'Mac's right,' Fox says. 'She's not a good friend, Cal. And it feels wrong just to let her walk back into our lives and think that's enough to make things right. That's like letting her off the hook.'

I don't answer. There's a hollowness in the air, a hollowness that always appears whenever Eli's mentioned. His absence is always here, but the space becomes even emptier when we draw attention to it.

'I don't want to talk about this anymore,' Mac says. 'Finn's coming back. Let's just eat lunch and act normal.'

And we do, and the unwritten rule is that we'll talk about Zelle in front of Finn, but not about Eli.

Finn plonks back down on the grass and tears into this sandwich, covering his mouth with his hand whenever he speaks or laughs, which is a lot. He has a nice laugh. Lyrical and bouncy. And those dimples. Those dimples you could sail boats in.

Ugh.

I add that to the list of things not to think about.

Fox and I have history together, but he stays behind after class since he and Mac have after-school choir practice. I'm heading home on my own when I see Finn standing by the school gates.

At first I think he's waiting for me, then I see he's on the phone. And he's not happy. We make eye contact, but he doesn't acknowledge me. I'm not sure what to do. It feels wrong to hang around, but it also feels wrong to walk away.

'I know. Sorry. Just not this weekend, okay? I only just got here.' He looks at the ground and kicks at a pebble as the person on the other end of the line keeps talking. He sighs. Loudly. 'I will. I *will*,' he says. 'All right. Okay. Bye. Love you too.' He rolls his eyes, slides his phone into his jacket pocket and shakes his head. 'Sorry,' he says.

'Who was that?' I say as we set off. I'm not usually so direct, but I have a feeling Finn would've asked if it had been me. In fact, he'd probably give me a three-minute unprompted speech about it.

'My mother.' He sighs. 'Already nagging me to come back to Alex for the weekend. As if I wasn't still living with her, like, two weeks ago.'

'I didn't know that,' I say.

'My parents split up a year ago,' Finn says. 'Mum said the house was hers so Dad's only option was a tiny rental cabin on the edge of town, which basically made the decision for who was going to look after me.'

I'm not sure how to respond, considering it sounds like a pretty heavy mess. But Finn seems unfazed. 'And then four months ago my mum's new boyfriend Bruce moves in. Such a bloke. Like, your classic boys-don't-cry-beer-drinking-tradie kind of bloke. Anyway, I can tell Bruce finds his loud, queer, half-Middle Eastern stepson a little too much to handle. He kept threatening to take me out trout fishing.'

'Horrible,' I say. (Queer? *Queer*?!) 'About the trout fishing, obviously.'

Finn laughs. 'I *know*. The straight white male energy was too much to handle. So when my dad got the job here, that was that.'

'Glad you got out of there, then,' I say. 'Though I have to say that Mistakesville isn't quite devoid of straight white male energy either.'

'I can't believe everyone really calls it that,' Finn says. 'Anyway. What about you? What's your family horror story?'

'Prepare to be disappointed,' I say. 'It's pretty tame. Just me, my mum and my sister. Kate was an accident with some one-night stand my mum hooked up with while doing her Master's, and Mum thought my sister could do with a sibling. I'm the product of a sperm bank. You can thank my anonymous sperm donor for my existence.'

'No way,' Finn says. 'That's amazing. Your mum sounds like a queen.'

I laugh. 'She is.'

'I need to meet this woman.'

'Easy,' I say. 'Still early days for meeting the parents.' It's only once it's out of my mouth that I realise how flirtatious that sounds.

I'm pretty sure I'm blushing.

I'm pretty sure Finn's blushing too.

'Sorry,' I say. 'That sounded bad.'

'No apology necessary.' His voice is light. 'That was weird today. With Zelle.'

We're only two houses away from mine.

(Why is this walk taking so long?)

'Yeah,' I say. 'I guess.'

'You two were best friends, huh?'

'Yeah.'

I can tell what question's brewing, so I answer before Finn can ask. 'We were always just friends,' I say. 'Nothing more. Everyone assumes we were, you know, but definitely not. No way. Never. Not my thing at all. Dating, I mean. Dating girls. Anyway. Ugh. I'll stop talking now.'

I want to crawl into a hole and die.

Finn is smirking at me.

'Understood,' he says. 'Sorry for asking.'

'Don't be,' I say.

He smiles. 'I thought you had work on Mondays?'

'I don't have set hours usually. It's mostly freelance. Last week was different because I had to interview somebody.'

'Who?'

'Tim Cooney. The councillor.'

'The bald guy?' Finn laughs. 'My dad says he's a wanker.'

'He *is* a wanker.'

'And you're writing about him?'

'Unfortunately, yes,' I say. 'Doing a feature on him, since local elections are coming up.'

'Poor you,' Finn says. Then he turns and saunters off down the street. 'Have fun writing about your wanker!' he calls.

Stakesville's Main Man: An Interview with Tim Cooney (second draft)

By Callum Rig

Councillor Tim Cooney has represented the Stakesville ward on the Central Otago Regional Council for the past three years. And now, with the local body elections coming up, he's hoping to serve for three more. But is he the right man to represent our changing town?

Tim Cooney is passionate about this corner of the world. When we meet in Perfect Mistakes café, Mr Cooney excitedly tells me about his achievements during his three years as our councillor. He's led projects to refurbish the Stakesville tourist information centre, built the new McCool Street community playground, and created better parking along the main road. But Cooney is also keenly aware of the challenges and obstacles our town faces, and believes it is crucial that these are front of mind for any councillor.

'I'm an optimist, not an idealist,' Cooney says. 'I'm realistic. I want the best for our town, but I'm also aware of the issues we face and how we need to get through them.'

Among Cooney's biggest concerns are a stalling local economy and a decreasing population, as more families leave for larger metropolitan areas and the remaining population grows older.

'Stakesville's a great place to grow up, and I think it's one of the best places in the world to raise a family,' Cooney says. 'Five generations of my family have grown up here, myself included, and there's so much to offer here that's unique to the area. We have affordable living, a close-knit community, a rich history, natural beauty. The list goes on.'

It's these qualities, Cooney says, that need to be utilised to maximise Stakesville's full potential. Cooney's top priorities, if elected for a second term, are to further invest in the tourism sector: an upgrade to the cycle trail and funding to create a gold rush museum are on the cards. Cooney has also proposed to invest $2 million to expand the Sunshine View Retirement Village.

'It's all about getting the economy moving. Quality investments lead to quality outcomes.'

When I ask Mr Cooney what he likes most about Stakesville, he tells me it's the people. 'The people, always the people,' he says. 'They are at the heart of this community. They know we come from a special place, and they help it thrive.'

However, Cooney's love of community appears to come with caveats. His personal opinions on the LGBTQIA+ community do not reflect his warm embrace of the people. In reference to the rainbow community, Mr Cooney said that 'they should have the freedom to do as they please, but there's no need to . . . show off about it [or] stick it in everyone's faces.'

Such a statement is a blatant display of homophobia. Tim Cooney's disgust at a community simply embracing who they are is obvious. His disparaging remarks show closed-mindedness and prejudice, and his community-centred approach loses all meaning when he refuses to show acceptance, care or even basic respect to the LGBTQIA+ group. Stakesville needs a strong-willed and visionary councillor to lead us into the future. But a councillor who wishes to deny the freedom of a long-oppressed group is stuck in the past. Homophobia and ignorant privilege are not what the Central Otago Regional Council needs.

[Document saved]

ZELLE

After Monday morning maths, I don't see Cal or the others again. And, because my last class is a study period, I'm able to leave at lunchtime.

Mum's waiting in the car outside the school gates.

'How was your day?' she asks.

'Okay,' I mumble.

And that's all.

Tuesday is a different story.

I have biology first, my favourite subject. As a kid I was a massive science freak. That's why I came up to Callum with the steelblue ladybird I'd found climbing up the doorframe on my first day at school. Steelblue ladybirds don't live in Europe, and it was the most splendid insect I'd ever seen. I had to share my discovery with someone. And when I looked at the sea of faces in the classroom and saw Callum I knew he was the one I'd share it with.

I could see he was friendly, but timid, reserved, nervy. I was homeschooled while we were travelling and I'd never really had any friends, but there was something about Cal that told me he was someone I wanted to bring the good side out of. Someone to take along on my adventures. And someone to drag down with me, since I knew he could never say no.

Anyway, when we moved to Wellington, I dropped the freakish science-nerd stuff in favour of friends and ditching class and meeting guys from the local boys' school. It's not that I ever really lost interest in science. It's more that I lost interest in trying.

That's how I felt about most things when we left Stakesville.

And the fact that no one will like you if you tell them your biggest interests are insects and arachnids.

As soon as I walk into biology, Mr Harrington hands me a folded slip of yellow paper. I read it right in front of him.

Giselle Bachmann, Year 13 biology, room J2

Please meet with Mr Appleby in room A9, if the time is convenient.

'What's this for?'

Mr Harrington shrugs. 'I'm not sure.'

'Who's Mr Appleby?'

'He's the guidance counsellor.'

Fuck me sideways.

'Do I have to go?' I say.

Mr Harrington smiles. 'Don't worry. I'll give you the

handouts now and the pages in the textbook to read. You won't miss much.'

As if that's why I was asking.

Once Mr Harrington's armed me with a stack of Punnett square questions and a reading on genetic mutations, I head out the door. My legs have turned to jelly. I seriously consider walking home. But ditching a trip to the counsellor is usually a sign that you probably *need* to be seeing a counsellor, and I don't want Mr Appleby, whoever he is, on my case for the rest of the year.

It's fine. I'm fine. I can prove it.

Mr Appleby's office is easy to find in the administration block. The door is slightly open, but I wait after I've knocked — I don't walk right in. I hear a chair creak and footsteps on the carpet.

'Hello,' he says. 'Giselle, is it? Come in. Take a seat.'

Shoot me now.

Mr Appleby has the saggy jowls and droopy eyes of those sad-looking dogs with the wrinkly faces. But he doesn't look sad, because he has a smile like Santa's. I slump into a scratchy red chair.

'Welcome, Giselle. I'm Mr Appleby, the guidance counsellor here.'

Does a bear shit in the woods?

'It's Zelle,' I say.

'Zelle. Right. Okay.' He folds one leg over the other. 'It's lovely to meet you, Zelle. I understand this isn't your first time in Stakesville, is it?'

I shrug, because what can I say? Is he competing for the

gold medal at making the most redundant conversation on earth?

'Are you from here originally?' Mr Appleby asks.

At least this is a question I can answer with actual words. 'I was born in Berlin,' I say. 'My dad's German, my mum is Dutch.'

Mr Appleby looks riveted.

'When did you come to Stakesville?' he asks.

'Not until I was nine,' I say. I hesitate, because the first nine years of my life are just one great big clump of *privilege*, and I don't know how to mention it without sounding like either a total prick or ungrateful. 'My parents are artists, so we used to travel a lot. We lived in Berlin until I was three, and then Brussels, and Paris, and Barcelona. And then, finally, here.'

Mr Appleby's eyes look ready to pop out of his head.

'*Amazing*,' he says. 'That must have been exciting for you.'

'Yeah,' I say, and of course it was great, but what I don't say is how it was also lonely, because Mum and Dad were always out at exhibitions and parties and events and I didn't have friends because I never stayed long enough in one place to make any. How, as much as I hate to admit it, Stakesville feels like my hometown more than anywhere, because it's the first place I belonged. Rooted myself. How when I was nine years old and a new immigrant, I felt like I didn't belong anywhere, and I feel the exact same way now.

Of course I don't say any of that.

But as if he can read my mind, Mr Appleby asks, 'What was it like to move to Stakesville?'

'Different,' I say. 'Small. Isolated, compared to where else we'd lived. But it also felt more connected. Community-like, I guess. My dad opened up his own gallery, so we met a lot of people.'

I know this will be the moment when Mr Appleby realises it. It's the same reaction everyone has. My dad is Walter Bachmann. *The* Walter Bachmann. The postmodern German artist, not the most famous in the world, but famous enough for his own Wikipedia page and for anyone who knows anything about art to know of him.

I wait for the inevitable *Oh my God, he's your DAD, what's it like being famous, blah blah blah*. The moment when I stop being me and become Walter Bachmann's daughter.

But that doesn't happen. Mr Appleby meets my eyes, and he nods, acknowledging what we both know. And then he moves on.

'I see you've been in Wellington the past three years,' he says. 'What was that like?'

'Cool. Fun. I had lots of friends.' I can't hide the resentment that creeps into my voice.

'It must have been difficult to leave,' he says. 'Especially at such short notice.'

'Yeah, well.'

'Do you like being back here?'

'Do you think I want to live in this shithole?'

He laughs, which is not an entirely unpleasant surprise. 'I suppose small-town living is an . . . acquired taste,' he says, gazing wistfully out the window at the field before turning his attention back to me. 'I'll be upfront with you, Zelle. Your mother has told me about your alcohol use and why you two left Wellington. It's confidential information, so nobody—'

'She told you?' I say, rising from my chair. 'Why the fuck did she tell you?'

He speaks as calmly as if we were talking about the weather, which just infuriates me more. 'Listen, Zelle, we respect that's private information. But it's also important information, and when we're worried about someone's wellbeing, sometimes we have to share sensitive stuff. The school admin had to know why you were leaving school in Wellington and what we could do to support you here. And we're hoping that talking with me might—'

'I do *not* have a drinking problem,' I say, swinging my bag onto my shoulder. 'And I don't need to talk about it.'

I make for the door.

'Zelle.'

I stop.

Mr Appleby is standing.

'I'm not making any judgements here,' he says. 'I'm not taking any sides. I want to hear *your* story.' He holds his hands up, as if in surrender. 'If you'll let me.'

'Well, I won't,' I say. 'Because there's nothing to talk about, so you and your nosy school admin can fuck off.'

I slam the door behind me. My hands tremble and my heart hammers. When I'm outside, I don't turn back to the science block, back to biology, back to school. I walk straight out of the grounds and onto the street. I consider going to Nicky's shop, but she'll call Mum for sure. And I'd rather confront her myself.

I run all the way home.

CALLUM

Zelle isn't at school on Tuesday.

I suppose it's not really my problem, but I still feel a tug of worry when during second period English Mrs Zaslavsky calls out Zelle's name on the roll and there's no response. Mrs Zaslavsky looks around the room, then shrugs, sighs and reads out the next name.

I glance at Finn and Fox (Mac has P.E. when we have English; she says she 'isn't a book person'), but they don't seem to notice, or care, about Zelle's absence, so I say nothing.

During maths is when I get properly worried.

'Isn't it weird that Zelle's not here?' I say.

Mac glowers at me as if I've just vomited all over her shoes. (Which I did do, once, after having too many vodka shots at her birthday last December.) 'I'm enjoying it, to be honest,' she says.

Which annoys me. I don't get annoyed very often. But now I am.

'She wasn't in English, either,' I say. 'Don't you think that's at least, like, a little concerning?'

Mac's look goes from sick-on-her-shoes intensity to sick-on-her-thousand-dollar-wedding-gown level. 'No,' she says, 'because it's not my business whether she's ditching school or what. You know what she's like, Cal. And I don't care.'

'It's only her second day,' I say.

'And? Why are you still going on about this?'

I match her glare. 'You're being heartless.'

Mac slaps her pencil on the table. 'Zelle doesn't have a heart, so why should I?'

I look at Fox for back-up.

'She's probably just doing it for attention,' he says solemnly.

My last hope is Finn.

He holds his hands up. 'I'm staying out of this,' he says. 'To be fair, though, if I were her, I wouldn't be too keen on coming to school and dealing with us either.' He shrugs.

'See?' Mac says. 'Let her carry on her melodrama. Maybe she'll finally stop when she realises no one's watching.'

'You don't know her like I do,' I mutter, and immediately regret it, because I can feel Mac's anger in the air like burning rubber.

'Is that so, Cal?' she says. 'Like how you *knew* she'd come back after what happened to Eli?'

I'm stunned at how easily Eli's name slips from her

mouth. I can tell Fox is too. Finn just looks confused, and I feel bad for letting him into our group right as everything is falling apart, plunging him into our chaos. I wonder if he wishes he was back in Alexandra. If we're even worse than a boring blokey cis-het stepdad.

'Sorry,' Mac says, immediately sensing the sour change in the air. 'It's just that she's already captured you under her spell once, Cal. And you're letting it happen again.'

Luckily for me, that's when Mr Abassi tells us that class is over. It's lunchtime now, and I get up, grab my bag and head straight out the classroom door.

'Where are you going?' Mac asks.

'To work on my article,' I lie, without turning around.

The corridor is flooded with students as classes slowly break out. I push my way through them and make my way outside, even though I don't have a clue where I'm going. After a few minutes of aimless walking, I decide to go home. I can afford to miss one lesson of media studies.

Descartes is napping on the concrete steps outside our front door, basking in the sunlight. He slips inside as I unlock the door.

'Ditching school?' Kate says.

I hold up my hands. 'Don't tell Mum.'

She grins. 'Don't tell her what?'

'You're the best.'

'Yeah, yeah.' She flops onto the couch. 'But I'm only keeping your secret if you watch Netflix with me.'

I roll my eyes and huff out a theatrical sigh. 'Fine.'

I shake my head and plonk down on the couch next to

her. She scrolls through options on the TV.

'Bad day?' she says.

'Yeah. Kind of.'

'Zelle?'

I glance at her from the corner of my eye. 'Yeah.'

'Want to talk about it?'

'No.'

We're almost halfway through the new season of our favourite trashy series when my phone pings. Mac's sent a message to our group chat.

OK, we've been talking and you have a point. You can invite Zelle to the party. We can have a truce, be open minded. This DOES NOT mean we're friends with her again tho.

Agreed, I write.

And I wonder if I'm doing the right thing.

ZELLE

'What the hell did you do?' I scream.

Mum is working on a new canvas. There's paint smeared on her face. 'Zelle!' Her brush clatters to the ground. 'Why aren't you in school?'

I am a tornado. A fuming storm in the shape of a girl. Mum told me that when I was born, Berlin was having its worst winter in years. I was brought into the world during a blizzard so harsh she and Dad almost didn't make it to the hospital because of the icy roads and city chaos. And I think part of that storm's always inside of me. That the ice burrowed under my skin, and I'll always be a flurry of snow and sleet and tempest.

'You told the school! You told me you'd keep it private and you told the fucking school!'

I'm barely coherent but Mum knows what I mean. She stands up, and she looks mad, but part of her looks fearful too. Which I find satisfying.

'Giselle,' she says. 'You need to go back to school. Right now. I'll drive you.'

'I don't have a drinking problem,' I yell.

Mum shakes her head. '*Liefje*,' she says softly, which startles me, because it's a Dutch term of endearment she hasn't used since I was about twelve. It's too gentle a word to describe me. 'You're not listening.'

'Why do you care so much?' I shriek. 'Why can't I get a break? It's not as if this is easy for me, you know.'

'Well, it's not easy for me either, Zelle.'

I laugh a laugh so hollow it rattles in the empty cavern where my heart should be. '*You* don't have to face the outside world,' I spit. '*You* don't have old friends to confront. *You* don't have a past to face. You've got it the *easiest* it could be. You're a hypocrite. You don't even leave the fucking house!'

Mum goes quiet, which is a surprise. Usually that happens only when she's really, really mad, which even for her is rare. The kind of mad where she'll turn around and tell me, calmly, that she wishes I wasn't her daughter or she wishes she could get rid of me. Last time she got that mad was the beginning of last year when Anahera and I got suspended for bringing vodka to school. Mum told me to get out of the house, which I did. I stayed the night at Anahera's — sneaking in through her window so her parents wouldn't know — until Mum called me the next day and said sorry and asked me to come home. That was back when Mum would actually *tell* me to get out, before I met Luka and the others and started drinking more. Now she barely lets me out of her sight.

So, anyway, I'm expecting Mum to do something like that: frog-march me into the car then dump me on the side of the road, maybe, or just tell me that she hates me. Instead, Mum's acidic-blue eyes go glassy, and my heart seizes in my chest as a tear rolls down her cheek.

She reaches up quickly to wipe it away. Then another falls. Then another. And before my anger has barely morphed into panic, Mum's sitting on the sofa, head in her hands, and she's crying.

I'm completely spooked. I don't know what to do. My mother always cries in secret. She cries behind closed doors. And she never, ever talks about it.

This is not how I thought things would go.

'What?' Sympathy isn't my strong suit, evidently, but I guess that runs in the family. I'm trying my hardest to make my voice go soft, but the effort only makes me sound harsher than ever.

Mum sniffs, blinks rapidly. 'The past is everywhere,' she says. 'All over this house. In every corner.' She drags her fingers under her eyes. '*He* is everywhere.'

She's talking about my dad, of course. Which I don't respond to. Not because I'm not sure what to say. Because that's something we don't talk about either.

My Wellington friends know that my parents are divorced and that my dad moved back to Berlin. They don't know that he lives there in a ritzy condo with his girlfriend who's half his age. Well, as far as I know: I haven't spoken to my dad in almost two years. Every few months he sends Mum his child support payments and then some. For my birthday and Christmas he puts the money straight into my bank account. He's never called. Neither have I.

'I want you to get better, Zelle,' Mum sniffs. 'Please try. Try to get better.'

'I'm fine,' I say softly. 'I haven't had a drink in three weeks, and I'm fine. I'm not dying of withdrawal.'

That's what happens to true addicts when they quit too quickly, isn't it? They die. And I'm most definitely not dead. And, even when I'm drinking, I'm still *functioning*. Like, I'm not wasting my days sleeping on the couch because I'm too wasted to do anything. When I've had a hard night, I just take a shot in the morning and get on with it. It's like magic.

Why doesn't anyone see that?

I'm fine.

I'm *fine*.

Mum's decided not to talk anymore, not even to tell me to go back to school, so I head to my room and stay there, lying on my bed with my eyes open, waiting for the day to end.

It's after four o'clock when my phone rings.

I sit up.

The only person who's likely to call me is Luka. And Luka never calls me first.

Hope rises in my chest.

It fizzles into confusion when I see the name on the screen: *Callum*.

I'm almost too scared to answer.

'Hello?'

'Hey,' he says. 'It's, um, it's Cal.'

'I know.'

Silence. Static.

'Still there, Zelle?'

'Yeah.'

'I was just calling because . . . because, y'know, you weren't at school today. And I was worried. So I'm just making sure you're okay. *If* you're okay.'

My heart tugs. I'm at once grateful and unworthy, pleased but befuddled. 'Yeah. Yeah. I'm fine. I just . . . wasn't feeling that well. Cold, maybe.' I sniff for effect.

'Oh. Oh, okay. That's good. Well, good that you're okay.'

I sniff again, but this time it isn't forced. 'Thanks.'

'Also . . . there's a party on this Friday? Joe Rooney's?'

'The woolshed party?' I say, remembering the revered yearly tradition. Only seniors are invited, but we'd been looking forward to the day for years. I was always itching to go.

'Yeah,' Cal says. 'So, anyway, that's on, and I've been talking to the others and . . . do you want to come?'

A party.

A party means a chance to socialise.

A chance to make things less awkward with the others.

A chance to feel normal.

A party means alcohol.

'Zelle?'

'Sorry,' I say. 'Yeah. Yeah, I'd love to come. That'd be great.'

'Okay.' He hesitates, and I kick myself for sounding so enthusiastic. 'Just so we're clear,' he says, 'this isn't, like, a sign that we're all best friends again and everything's fine. There's still a long way to go with that. But I hope this can be a start. An extending of the olive branch, if you will.' He sucks in a breath. 'God, that was cringe.'

I laugh. 'Don't worry,' I say, giggling because I know that three years ago Cal would have said something that awful *unironically*. He's always been full of antique idioms like *don't be daft* and *pot calling the kettle black* and *put that in your pipe and smoke it*. It's a relief to know that part of him's still there.

'I can pick you up on Friday night,' Callum says. 'We'll drop the car at mine and walk the rest of the way to Joe's. It's only twenty minutes up the hill. Eight sound good?'

'Eight is fine,' I say.

The static stings with a growing awkwardness. 'Great,' he says. 'I'll see you then. Bye, Zelle.'

'Bye, Cal.'

He hangs up first.

I flop back onto my pillow.

I throw my phone on the duvet.

And I smile, because it's the first time I've felt this close to Callum in three years.

CALLUM

Zelle's cold seems to have miraculously cleared up overnight, because she's back at school the next day and looking bright as ever. She sits at our table during maths again, and everyone makes an attempt to be civil, though Fox is as stiff as a marionette and Mac looks as if being nice physically pains her. Finn doesn't ignore Zelle, but he doesn't make an active effort to talk to her either. Mostly because he's always talking to me. That boy's mouth is a motor that never stops.

She doesn't join the four of us at lunchtime and keeps her distance for the rest of the week. I'm not sure where she goes, but there seems to be an unspoken agreement that none of us will seek her out.

On Friday afternoon I'm walking to last-period media studies when she comes down the corridor towards me. My chest flutters with the reflexive Zelle-induced anxiety, but she throws a shy smile my way, and I smile back without even forcing myself to.

And for the first time in three years, things feel somewhat normal between us.

ZELLE

Mum says there's no way I'm going to Joe Rooney's party.

'It's not a good idea, Zelle,' she says, over and over again, until she sounds like her broken Joni Mitchell vinyl that always gets stuck on the chorus during 'A Case of You'.

'There won't be alcohol,' I say.

She raises a disbelieving eyebrow.

'Please,' I say. 'How am I ever meant to do better if I'm not even allowed to have fun?'

'There are other ways to socialise,' she says, obviously forgetting that we live in the literal armpit of the earth and that this party is the only social event on the Stakesville calendar. 'I'm not budging, Zella. No parties.'

I stomp to my room and text Cal.

Can u please pick me up from the end of the driveway?

The three typing dots dance across my screen.

sure . . . see you at 8 still?

I send a thumbs-up emoji.

And then I get ready for Joe Rooney's party.

It's different from how it usually is when I go out. I've no friends here to share the moment with. There's no music pouring out of speakers, first drink in hand as we get dressed up, borrowing each other's clothes and doing each other's makeup. In the sullen quiet of the house I put on black vinyl pants and a white cropped shirt — chic but understated — and do my makeup in the full-length mirror I bought from Nicky's shop last weekend, since I couldn't bring mine from home. With my friends it usually takes us an hour or more to get ready; by myself, I'm done in twenty minutes. I even straighten my hair for something to do.

At 7.50 I open the latch on my bedroom window and let it swing out wide. I grab my jacket off the door hook and shrug it on. It's Luka's jacket — he lent it to me one night when we were drinking at the beach with the others. When I tried to give it back, he refused to take it.

'You keep it,' he told me. 'It looks better on you.'

I pull one leg over the sill, then the other, and land on the grass with a soft *thump*. I wait to see if Mum's heard me before I dare to move again. The night stays still and quiet, so with mouse footsteps I creep round the side of the house and up to the gates of The Sanctuary. Once I'm at the driveway, I run.

Callum's car is waiting for me.

And the others are inside.

'Hey,' Mac says as I climb into the left-side backseat. She's sitting shotgun. Her voice is completely unfriendly. 'What's up with the incognito pick-up? You sneaking out?'

Fox is sitting next to me, Finn on his right. I can feel both their eyes on me. My skin starts to prickle.

'No,' I say, clenching my jaw. 'Our driveway is under works at the moment. Super-potholed. Uneven. Thought I'd save Cal the inconvenience.'

'I'm sure he wouldn't have minded,' Mac says, turning her head to face him. He keeps his eyes fixed on the road. 'Eh, Cal?'

'No big deal.' He shrugs. I can tell he's uncomfortable.

'What are you drinking, Zelle?' Mac says pointedly, taking in the fact I've come empty-handed.

I want to yell at her to stop being such a bitch, but Cal invited me to the party to try to make peace and the others agreed, so I should be grateful I'm getting the chance to talk to Mac at all. I plaster on my brightest, fakest smile, even though it rattles my teeth.

'I have work tomorrow,' I say, which at least is the truth. 'So I thought I'd better not have anything. Don't want to be hungover at work.'

'Didn't think that would stop you,' she says. 'You've never really been a consequences person, have you?'

'Mac,' Fox warns. 'Chill out. This is meant to be a fun night. Don't make this hard.'

Mac looks like she wants to throttle him, but then she huffs out a sigh and flops back into her seat. She's silent as we pull up outside Callum's house.

I try to send Fox a silent thanks, but he won't look at me.

We pile out of the car like kids on a family road-trip and begin the walk up to Joe's. Mac and Cal are each holding a bottle of those cheap one-litre ciders that taste like sour piss, while Fox – a true Otagonite – carries a crate of beer, and Finn brandishes a bottle of cleanskin wine that definitely came from the bottom shelf of the supermarket. Everyone's made an effort for tonight, with slicked-back hair and starchy shirts, clothes too good to wear to school. It's a scene I know all too well, but the air doesn't fizz like it's meant to. It feels like we're on a funeral march. Not on our way to a party everyone's been looking forward to the entire year.

Mac and Fox lead the pack, talking quietly. Cal and Finn are behind them, also chattering, by which I mean Finn blabbers excitedly and laughs and throws his hands around, while Cal mumbles replies and progressively shrinks to the size of a flea.

He's definitely got a crush.

If things were the way they were before, I'd tease him about it. Be his wingman. Force him to get his act together and make a move, because I know he will never be able to do it himself. As we near the lip of the hill to Joe's farm, Cal and Finn stop and wait for me.

'All right?' Cal says.

'All good,' I lie.

'They're trying,' he says, though I'm finding that increasingly hard to believe. It feels like I'm watching the others' lives play out as a movie and I'm stuck on the wrong side of the cinema screen.

The party is loud and thrumming and *big*. The woolshed is decked out with fairy lights and a stereo with a thumping bass I can feel inside my skull. Literally everyone from our year group is here, plus some friends of Joe's older brothers and a couple of Year Twelves who must have enough connections to be allowed in. It's so much like the parties from home that for a moment I feel like I'm right there back in Wellington. Apart from the hay bales and silos everywhere, and the southern-tinged accents, and the smell of sheep shit.

And there's a lot of alcohol.

Everyone's holding a bottle of wine or beer or cider or a can of RTD. There's a table set up with a stack of red plastic cups and a jug of what looks like sangria that appears to be for everyone.

My hands clench into fists at my side.

Here's the thing: parties just aren't the same when you're sober. There's no dancing like you don't care who's watching, because you don't, or telling your life story to a stranger or kissing a stranger or lying back on the grass and watching the stars spin.

Life without alcohol is boring.

The others have already joined a group who've made themselves at home in a corner. They're sprawled over the hay bales, laughing and talking and drinking.

I take a deep breath, then wander over.

'Hey,' I say, sounding about as relaxed as a Seventh Day Adventist at a warehouse rave. 'What have I missed?'

'Zelle Bachmann!' Joe Rooney's plastered already. 'Where have you been the past three years?'

'Oh, you know,' I say, which is thankfully enough of an answer, because Joe's already forgotten he's even asked me a question. He looks at my empty hands with eyes wide. 'Why aren't you drinking anything?'

'She's working tomorrow,' Mac says. 'Being very responsible.'

I want to slap the smirk off her face.

'What about a sangria? I made it myself. It's good shit, let me tell you.'

Finn points at Callum. 'Is that the sangria that—'

'We're not talking about that,' he says, and everyone laughs, and I wait for someone to let me in on the joke, but they don't, and I feel like a fool sitting here when it's obvious I don't belong and no one *wants* me to belong.

'C'mon, Zelle,' Joe says. 'At least have one.'

Mac's judgement burns holes into my back.

Just one. Just one drink. Then I can be like everybody else and at least enjoy myself a bit more.

'Joe!' Miri Waitere is staggering over, and practically collapses into Joe's arms. A couple? This is news to me. She looks at me through sleepy, heavy eyes.

'Hi, Zelle,' she drawls. 'I like your hair.'

'Oh. Thanks,' I say, but the conversation has moved on already, and soon I'm lost in the tide of drunken conversation and mindless shouting and the throb of the bass and the party getting louder and louder and louder. I can't get in a word in, partly because I can't follow the thread of the conversation, and partly because everyone's shouting over each other anyway and I'm not pissed enough to join in. The way Fox and Mac have positioned themselves, backs turned and forming a tight circle, means I'm on the periphery. Left out.

I wanted to feel normal, but now I wish I'd never come.

While Joe and Miri start making out and everyone boos, I get up. Mac clearly notices, but she doesn't say anything, and I want more than ever to deck her across the face. I turn and head for the entrance. The sangria set-up beckons; I think about filling a cup and sitting on the hill, watching the stars, watching the party unfold without me.

'Zelle.'

I jump as a hand touches my arm.

Cal's cheeks shine pink with alcohol and his eyes glitter behind his glasses. Obviously I've never seen Callum drunk before, but with his confused face and slack arms and drink dangling limply from his hand he looks like a little kid.

'Where are you going?' he says, and stupidly, for no reason at all, I feel tears prick like needles behind my eyes.

And that's it.

'Oh, so now you care?' I snap, and Cal recoils like I've just hit him. His mouth hangs open.

'What?'

'Why did you even ask me to come?' I yell, aware of people starting to look, including our group. 'It's obvious no one wants me here.'

'Finally, some awareness,' Mac whispers to Fox, but not quietly enough, deliberately not quietly enough.

Cal looks down at the ground. 'I'm trying, Zelle,' he says.

'Well, no one else is,' I say, and I'm looking straight at Mac. She stands up too.

'Because why would we?' Mac says. 'You did the shittiest thing you could have done and then disappeared to Wellington and left us all behind. And *now* you come back here and decide to be part of our lives again because *now* it suits you, and you expect us to let you back in that easily? You really think we *want* to be friends with you after what you did?'

'I'm not the only one to blame,' I say, and my blood is boiling and my words are falling straight from my mouth without even going through my brain. 'Your precious Callum isn't an angel, you know. Maybe he ought to finally tell you how dating Eli is what started the tension in the first place.'

There's silence now, a silence so heavy it hangs over us like lead, and I watch as Mac and Fox gape and gawk at Callum for confirmation and he just shrugs slowly. Then his head lifts up, and his gaze on mine is fuelled with terror — and something else. Something fierce. Something I haven't seen since the summer we turned fourteen.

Hatred.

And I know I really, really shouldn't have said that.

CALLUM

At first I think I'm dreaming.

Everything around me has gone very, very quiet. But my head is louder than ever, echoing with Zelle's words and thrumming from nerves and probably slightly too much alcohol. I look over at Fox and Mac, jaws dropped in disbelief. Joe and Miri, still tangled up in each other, gape too. And sitting haplessly in the middle, eyes asking a hundred questions, is Finn.

And then finally I look up at Zelle.

She paces the floor in deranged semi-circles, her hands wringing themselves into knots. Her face is pale and her eyes are wide. I can see the regret everywhere.

'Cal,' she says. 'I'm so sorry—'

'Don't.' I'm surprised how strong my voice comes out. 'Just don't, Zelle.'

And I run straight out of there.

I don't know where I'm going, but I don't stop.

Joe's farm is all hills and green grass and everything looks the same. I feel like I'm trapped in one of those dreams I sometimes have where I'm running but not actually moving. Zelle's voice plays loops in my head.

Dating Eli is what started the tension in the first place.

No one knows about me and Eli, apart from Zelle. Well, *knew*. Eli always wanted to keep us a secret: he wasn't ready for others to know yet, he said, he was still figuring things out. Me and Zelle had drifted apart that summer, so she didn't know about Eli until I finally told her. That just splintered us further apart, and then after what happened I didn't want to say anything to anyone else. It was too painful to talk about. The Famous Five had already been fractured and I didn't want to break it more.

'Callum!'

It's Finn's voice.

I turn around but I don't stop.

He jogs a little faster.

'Where are you going?'

I don't answer.

The terrain's rough and uneven, rugged country land. My balance is off-kilter and I'm an accident waiting to happen but I don't want to stop, despite how much of a massive dork I must look right now. (I've always been uncoordinated at the best of times, and it's not something anyone needs to see.) I can feel Finn catching up.

'Callum,' he says. 'You're about to be upside-down in a minute.'

'I don't care,' I mumble.

'Careful. If you trip over and die, I don't want to be held responsible for not stopping you. Imagine how bad that would look on my record.'

I keep stumbling down the hill.

'If you get yourself killed, I'll make sure to play shit songs at your funeral. Everyone will walk out. You'll only be remembered as the guy who was buried six feet under to Nickelback.'

I stop so abruptly that Finn walks right into me. I shove him away.

'Jesus, what was that for?'

'Fuck off, Finn!'

But he catches me just as my body gives way and my stomach lurches, and the horrors of tonight come back up. He smooths my hair off my forehead as I throw up all over Joe Rooney's sheep station.

Then he squats down next to me and gently rubs my back. 'Thanks for breaking my ribs, Callum,' he says. 'I didn't know Nickelback was such a sore point for you.'

'Stop being so dramatic.'

'Stop being a dick or I'll leave you here to freeze.'

I'm sitting with my knees pulled up, my arms wrapped tight around my legs. I drop my head onto my knees and groan.

'I think I'd prefer that,' I drawl.

Finn shuffles nearer and puts an arm around me. His body is warm, and I press a little closer against him.

'I'm sorry for what happened back there,' he says.

I grunt.

'I'm guessing Zelle wasn't supposed to say that.'

I grunt again.

'Is it because you're not out?' he says.

I lift my head and look at the stars. 'Not that,' I say. I've been out since I was thirteen: at the age when Kate started teasing me about girls, about Zelle, and I realised I couldn't make myself feel attracted to Zelle, or girls in general, and I probably never would. 'They know I like guys. But they didn't know about Eli.' I huff. 'It's complicated.'

'Seems like it,' he says.

'I never told them because I don't want to talk about it.'

He shifts to face me. 'Seems like you'll have to someday, though. Now that Zelle's back.'

I shrug. 'Sometimes the past should stay in the past,' I say, even though I know that's bullshit.

'You guys don't really talk about Eli,' Finn says. It's a statement but I know there's a question behind it.

Which I choose not to answer.

'Your hand's still on my back,' I say instead.

Finn looks startled, like he wasn't even aware he was still drawing lazy circles on my spine. 'Do you want me to take it off?' he says.

'No,' I say. 'Leave it.'

So he does. We go silent again.

His arm drops from mine as we hear Fox and Mac call out our names.

We're flooded in a golden wash of torchlight. Fox and Mac run towards us, two pinpricks of light hurtling closer like falling stars.

'There you are,' Fox says. 'We were getting worried.'

'Is that yours?' Mac says, pointing her torch at the patch of vomit stewing on the grass. She leans closer. 'Why is it so *chunky*? Don't you chew your food?'

'Are you okay?' Fox says, shining torchlight straight into my eyes.

I hold up an arm to block the light. 'Not particularly.'

'We're not mad, by the way,' Mac says, sitting down next to me. 'Just surprised, I guess. And maybe a little bit hurt.'

'I'm sorry,' I say.

Fox joins us on the ground, crouching opposite me. 'It makes sense that Zelle would know,' he says, not angrily but resigned. Even though it was obvious me and Zelle were best friends, I know the others still felt excluded.

'Where is Zelle?' I ask.

Fox rolls his eyes. 'Callum,' he says, 'you're lying in the middle of a field, you're drunk, there's vomit on your shoes, and your most pressing concern is the whereabouts of the person who just screwed you over, again.'

'There is?' I say, craning my neck to examine the state of my Converse. Which are, in fact, splattered with sick.

'I thought telling you would ruin the vibe,' Finn says, pointing at my shoes.

'She ran off not long after you left,' Mac interrupts. It takes my muddled brain a second to realise she means Zelle. 'Back home, I'm guessing.'

Of course. The events of the last half hour flood back:

Zelle sitting on the fringe of our group, getting more and more irritated as our conversation carried on without her. Her walking away. Me walking after her. What she said. The silence.

I don't know why I brought her here. I don't know what I expected. Things will never be the same, and it's impossible to pretend, even for one night, that we're okay. How could I be so naïve as to think I could ever trust her the way I once did? Like Fox said: she's screwed me over, again.

Stupid of me to think she might have changed.

The sinking of my mood must be visible on my face, because next thing I know Mac's looping an arm around me and Fox is doing the same, until we're huddled in a clumsy, lopsided group hug.

'Come on, you,' Mac says to Finn. 'You're invited.'

A flutter of warmth returns to my body as I feel Finn's weight against mine.

'Everything'll be okay,' Mac says.

'Seconded,' Fox says.

'Thirded,' Finn says. 'If that's a word.'

'Thanks,' I say, even though none of us believe it. I don't know if an empty promise is better than no promise at all, but at least the thought is a comfort.

We stay wrapped up in our human sandwich a while longer — long enough to begin to notice the smell of sheep, and sheep shit, and vomit.

Finn's the first to break free from our huddle.

'I know this is cosy and all,' he says, 'but can we get out of this fucking farm?'

ZELLE

I know I've ruined everything.

It's almost 1 a.m. by the time I get home. I run all the way, and it's exhausting, but I don't stop. I don't bother sneaking through my window and instead burst through the front door, not caring how much noise I make. Mum is up, anyway. Waiting for me.

'And where have you been?' she says, getting up from the couch. 'You didn't go to the party, did you?'

'Can we leave this for tomorrow?' I say.

She storms towards me. 'Have you been drinking?'

'No!'

She tilts my chin up, places her nose close to my lips to smell if there's alcohol on my breath. She pats down my jacket and shoves her hands in the pockets.

'Get off me!' I yell, trying to push her away. 'I *told* you, I haven't been drinking!'

She steps back, her arms folded, a pose I've come to know well over the past three years. 'And do you think I can trust you?' she says.

'You are such a bitch!' I shriek. 'I can't wait till I turn eighteen and can move out, you know. So that I can get away from you.'

'How dare you.'

'It's your fault everything's ruined,' I say, turning to leave. 'Maybe if you'd tried harder, Dad wouldn't have run off with someone else.'

I storm out of the room, knowing full well that once again I have made my mother cry. In my bedroom, door closed, I kick at my bed until the mattress springs screech and the wooden frame creaks. Once I've exhausted myself, I slide under the covers without even bothering to take my clothes off. I'm still in Luka's jacket, and I try to breathe in his smell, but tonight all my nostrils pick up is woodsmoke and the tang of regret.

I know, without a doubt, that Callum hates me now. He deserves to. So does Mum, and she doesn't even know what I did to Cal. Neither do Fox and Mac. No one knows the pure, ugly truth, except for Cal. And me.

It's my fault I ruined our friendship. It's my fault I broke everyone's trust.

And it's my fault that Eli's dead.

ZELLE

Work the next day sucks.

To put it lightly.

I'm barely two hours into my shift and I never want to see another antique knick-knack ever again. My head pounds from lack of sleep and hours spent crying. It's like a hangover, but worse.

'Come on, Zelle,' Nicky scolds me. 'I'm not paying you to stare into space and do nothing.'

'That's because there's nothing to do,' I fire back.

'Nonsense. There's always something. Like that crockery stocktake I asked you to do an hour ago.'

I glower at her. 'Why don't *you* do it?'

'Because I'm paying *you* to,' Nicky snaps. 'Which is our agreement, lassie, and if you don't want to partake then you can take your services elsewhere.'

I flush pink with the shame of being talked back to.

But then, to my surprise, Nicky disappears into the back room and re-emerges with a steaming cup of tea and a plate of shortbread. She hands me the mug and puts the shortbread on the counter.

'Well, go on. It's not poisonous.'

I blink myself back into reality and reach for a biscuit.

I'm not really a tea drinker, but Nicky's brew is rich and comforting, milky but not too sweet, just how I like it. The shortbread is perfectly buttery and soft, and it fills my mouth with homemade sweetness and nostalgia. I haven't had breakfast today, or coffee, and realise I'm ravenous.

'I'll get you some water,' she says as soon as I'm done. 'Anything else?'

'Why are you doing this for me?' I say. I know what I should be saying is *thank you*, but I can't quite form the words.

Nicky shrugs. 'I can tell something's up, lassie. Can practically smell it on you. What is it?'

It's embarrassing how easily she can read me. And how much of a train wreck I must look. 'Oh, nothing,' I say. 'Just . . . friend troubles.'

'Callum?'

I arch an eyebrow. I wonder for a moment if Nicky has psychic powers. I wouldn't put it past her.

I don't answer. Which means yes.

'What happened?' she says.

I pick at the scabbed-over grazes on my hand – my souvenir from almost being run down by Cal – as I think how to answer. 'I messed up,' I say. 'I did something bad.

Something unforgivable.'

Nothing more unforgivable than what I've already done, I think.

'Unforgivable's a strong word,' she says. 'It's pretty rare that something's that bad. Especially with two friends so tight. Like I've said before, you and Callum were like two beans in a pod.'

'*Peas*.'

'Do you know that for certain, anyway?'

'That it's *peas* in a pod?'

'That he won't forgive you?'

'Well.' I think about it for a moment. 'I haven't spoken to him.'

'Then speak to him, lassie,' Nicky says. 'You have to try first.'

'But I . . . I don't know if he even *wants* to talk to me.'

'Then find out. If your friendship means that much to the both of you, then you should be doing everything you can to make it right. And so should he.'

I don't want to massage Nicky's ego into believing she's some kind of all-knowing, advice-giving oracle, but she's right. Even without her knowing the full story, what she's saying is what's been stewing in my head all morning. I need to see Cal. And soon. I don't want to start another three years of silence. And even if he hates me, even if he shuts the door in my face and vows never to speak to me again, then I need to find that out for myself. I need to make it right. And if I can't, then I need to know that at least I tried.

Nicky heads for the back room.

'Where are you going?' I say.

'To call your mum.'

'What? Why?'

Mum and I have barely spoken since last night. She drove me to work in harsh, frosted silence. When I said *See you later*, she looked out the window and sniffed.

'To let her know there's extra work at the store today and to pick you up from your shift at four instead. So that at three o'clock you can go and speak to Callum.'

'I'm not sure that's a good idea—'

But she's off.

It's happening.

She's back less than two minutes later. 'That's all sorted,' she says. 'Now go do the ceramics stocktake. And you can think of what to say to Callum.'

She starts organising a box of new donations. Like a robot with a new battery, I finally spring into life.

'Thank you,' I say as I head towards the ceramics shelves.

Nicky looks up. 'I thought I'd never see the day,' she says.

CALLUM

It's almost midday by the time I finally drag myself out of bed and into the shower. My body feels like it's been laid with bricks, and my memories of last night are tinted in a drunken sheen.

I still remember everything, though. I wish I didn't.

I turn the water pressure up and try to drown out the memories.

It doesn't work. Zelle, in all her blue-haired, yellow-Docs glory is there every time I close my eyes, her soft, curious accent louder than the stream of the shower.

Cal, I'm so sorry.

'Sorry' never quite cuts it for Zelle.

I don't know how long I'm in the bathroom for, but it's long enough that my skin turns scallop pink and my fingers are soft and pruned. I put on my glasses, throw on fresh clothes (waking up in last night's outfit made me feel a particular kind of *ick*) and decide to face the outside world.

Which is where I'm faced with Finn.

Sitting at our kitchen table.

With Descartes on his lap.

He grins. 'Welcome to the land of the living.'

And my wrung-out body feels ready to explode.

'Want coffee?' he says. 'Your mum's about to make some.' His smile turns into a frown. 'If she's able to. You might've used up the town's entire water supply. Possibly the whole region's.' He pushes a plate of toast and a tall glass of water towards me. 'Your mum told me you like peanut butter. Sorry it's gone cold. I didn't know you were setting a world record for the longest shower in human history.'

I slump into a seat at the table, wondering if I'm dreaming. Or hallucinating. Or still drunk. Or in another universe.

'How did you get here?' I say when I can finally muster the brain power to make speech.

Finn smirks (God, that smirk is *lethal*) and quirks an eyebrow. 'You do remember I live about two minutes down the street from you? Maybe one and a half if you're in a rush.'

I take a bite of toast. It's cold and slightly stale, but it still tastes like magic, and I practically inhale the whole plateful. I can see Finn struggling not to laugh.

'I was just checking in,' he continues. 'Making sure you weren't dead.'

'I'm not dead.'

'I can see that,' he says. His gaze is so intense, it's like being shot with lasers. I'm extra-aware of how much of a mess I must look right now. He drops the smirk and his face turns serious. 'Are you okay?' he says in such a way that I know I won't be able to get away with a half-arsed answer.

But for once the universe seems to be working in my favour, because that's when Mum walks in.

'Back from the dead, Callum?'

I can feel a blush creeping up my neck. 'Apparently so,' I say.

Her grin is all too knowing. 'I'll make coffee,' she says, and puts the jug on to boil. She grabs the tin of coffee grounds from the cupboard. 'Good night?' she asks, her back still turned.

'Yeah,' I say, briefly glancing at Finn. 'It was fun.'

'Glad to hear it. More coffee, Finn?'

'Please,' he says, and his teeth shine like a string of pearls. Mum is definitely charmed. She puts three heaping scoops of grounds into the plunger and adds the just-boiled water. Even though it's the interruption I wanted, it's awkward now with Mum in the room. (Well, awkward for me, at least — Mum and Finn seem just fine.)

'I didn't hear you get back last night,' she says. She's leaning against the kitchen counter now, her dressing gown pulled tight around her. 'Finn says it was around one when you got back, wasn't it?'

'I think so,' I say.

'Did Zelle have a good time?'

If Mum can feel the tension at the mention of Zelle's name, she doesn't say so. 'Yeah. Yeah, I think she did,' I say.

'Did she get home okay? The Sanctuary's pretty far from town, isn't it?'

'The Sanctuary?' Finn asks.

'Zelle's house,' I say.

'The Sanctuary used to be an art gallery,' Mum says. 'Her parents are artists.'

'Don't bore him with the details, Mum.'

'Hold on,' Finn says, and his eyes widen as realisation dawns on him. *The* realisation. 'They're not — they're not *the* Bachmanns, are they? *Walter* Bachmann?'

I really, really want to stop talking about this, but Mum has other plans. 'That's them,' she says. 'They brought a pretty fair bit of attention to Stakesville back in the day.'

'Holy fucking shit,' Finn says, before pulling a face at Mum. 'Sorry.'

She grins. 'Don't worry. We're not strict on language here.'

Finn looks at me while he points at her. 'Do you know how lucky you are?' he says, mouth agape, which makes Mum burst into laughter. As charming as a spell on a snake.

Jesus.

'Is the coffee ready?' I say.

Mum presses the plunger down and fills up three mugs. 'Come get yours,' she says. 'The milk's on the counter.'

Finn leaps up and grabs a mug for him and a mug for me before I have the chance to do it myself. He pours milk into the first cup and holds the carton towards me like a salute. 'Milk?'

'Just a splash.'

He drops in a splash — quite literally, because droplets decorate the countertop like beads of sweat — and wipes it up before Mum even notices (and inevitably offers to clean it up herself, because that's the type of person she is). 'Enough?' he says.

'Perfect.'

He walks over, carrying the two cups. 'My room?' I say before he has a chance to put them down. I say it like a question but without room for an answer.

'Lead the way,' he says.

I begin shutting the door to my room out of habit, then worry that it might make Finn uncomfortable, so leave it open, then worry that that might make Finn *more* uncomfortable, so I stand facing the door overthinking what I should do until Finn laughs in a way that makes me want to crawl into a hole and die.

'What are you arguing with the door about?' he says. He's already made himself at home on my bed, sipping his coffee with his back against the wall. My mug's on the bedside table.

I turn and point to the door. 'Open or closed?'

'Closed is fine,' he says. 'I can jump out your window if you pull a knife on me. Drink your coffee. It'll cure your hangover.'

I sit next to Finn and take a sip of my coffee.

'Why did no one tell me Zelle's dad is Walter fucking Bachmann?' he says. 'We studied his work in art class last year. I saw his exhibition in Dunedin a couple years ago. He's literally iconic.'

'Out of everything to do with Zelle, the fact her parents happen to be famous didn't really seem important in the grand scheme of things,' I say. It comes out grouchier than I intended. But I also feel grouchier than I probably need to be.

'Sorry,' Finn says. 'It's just kind of, you know, a surprise. Changes the story a little bit.' I can tell he's choosing his words carefully, which is such an un-Finn-like thing to do that it makes it all the more obvious when he's doing it. 'Anyway. I know it's trivial. Sorry.'

'No big deal.'

A pause.

I finish the last dregs of my coffee to fill in the silence.

Finn says, cautiously, 'Can you forgive Zelle? For what she did last night?'

I can't give him an answer, because I don't have one.

Or maybe I do. But I don't want to admit it. Because admitting it would drain away every last dash of hope I've ever had that Zelle would come back to me. Admitting it would prove that I've been wrong about her this entire time.

'Just ask,' I say.

'Huh?'

'I know you want to ask about Eli,' I say. 'So just ask.'

He holds his hands up. 'You don't have to, if you don't want to,' he says. He sounds sincere, but I can tell by the glint in his eyes that he's curious.

I lie back on the bed. A river of sunlight washes in, its heat making me sleepy in a nice way. I take off my glasses, place them on the windowsill and rest a hand across my face.

My mattress creaks, and I can feel Finn's weight as he lies down next to me.

'Is this okay?' he says.

'Of course,' I say.

There's no sound apart from the faint rustle of the trees (Descartes doing his business, probably), and the pull of my and Finn's breathing. He breathes in as I breathe out, cyclical, rhythmic, our breathing getting slower as the minutes pass. I feel the tension from my body melt. My chest rises long and full, like a balloon, and falls like bricks from a building.

I swivel my neck towards Finn. Without my glasses even his shape is blurry, his details dulled and fuzzy. Sensing me looking at him, he looks over at me, and my reflex is to turn away, embarrassed for having him catch me staring. But there's something in his look that lets me hold his gaze.

I try to think of something to say. I can tell Finn's thinking too. But after a silent few moments we give up and just look at each other.

It's nice to look at him, uninhibited, even with my vision blurred. I consider reaching for my glasses, but I don't want to move. It feels like we're frozen in time and I don't want to break the spell.

I haven't dated anyone since Eli. Haven't kissed anyone since then. Never even *liked* anyone after him – not anyone I could have a proper crush on, anyway. We were friends since we were small, and he was always just Eli, until he was more. Until I realised I didn't like girls and what that truly meant. Until I found my gaze fixed on him all the time and I couldn't stop thinking about his face, his laugh, his smile, his clothes, his hair, his hobbies, the way I felt like I could listen to him forever and be perfectly content not to speak ever again—

'Eli's dead,' I say.

And the moment is over.

I turn to the wall so I don't have to see Finn's reaction.

'He was our friend. Everyone called us the Famous Five. Me, Zelle, Mac, Fox and Eli. He died in January, when we were fourteen. The weekend before school started. He was swimming alone in the lake. And he drowned.'

When I finally turn back to look at Finn, his eyes are wide.

'Oh, shit,' he says. 'I'm so sorry, Callum.' He sighs, then rolls his eyes. 'I know that's a pretty meaningless response. There's just nothing you can say to really make it better, though, is there?'

His earnestness nudges a dim smile out of me. 'No,' I say. 'Not really.'

'Were you—' Finn falters. 'Were you two dating? When he died?'

I sit up. The sun hits my back, but suddenly I feel cold. I draw my knees up to my chest and wrap my arms around myself.

'It was messy,' is all I can say, and I bite my lip and blink quickly until the tightness in my chest goes away. Finn sits silently next to me, but it's not the pleasant, contented silence we had before. This quiet is heavy. Awkward. Almost as if the last five minutes never happened.

'I should probably go,' Finn says. He looks at me. 'Do you want me to?'

I shrug. 'I'm exhausted. I'll probably go back to sleep,' I say.

'So, in other words, yes?' He's smiling.

'It's nothing to do with you,' I say softly.

'I know. No offence taken. You deserve to sleep.' He stands up. 'I'll see you Monday?'

'See you on Monday.'

He opens the door. 'Bye, Cal.'

He goes.

I fall back onto the bed.

I crawl under the covers.

But I can't sleep.

ZELLE

I'm pretty sure this is a terrible idea.

I'm standing on Callum's doorstep, my hands shoved deep into my pockets. I've already knocked, and while I still have time to run away I try to convince myself that what I'm doing is the right thing.

I'm having doubts, though.

A text apology wouldn't have cut it. An Instagram DM wouldn't be much better (we don't even follow each other), and a Facebook apology would be just as bad (we're definitely, definitely not Facebook friends). So really, I try to tell myself as I wait outside Cal's door, heart thundering, Nicky was right. I had no choice but to come here.

I wish I believed that.

When the door finally does open, I'm a thread of sanity away from bolting into the bushes. Kate's standing in the doorway.

She doesn't look happy to see me. To say the least.

Kate's always intimidated me, to be honest. The five years she had on us felt like a whole lifetime when we were kids. She was always friendly, and she and Cal have always been close, but she was cool and inaccessible in a way that made me uncomfortable. I haven't seen her since she was nineteen, when she was home from uni for the summer. She looks older, obviously, chiselled out. Her hair's changed, too: her amazing long hair's been cropped to a shaggy bob that barely hits her shoulders. There's a pang in my heart at seeing it short. Her long hair was so *Kate*.

I'm vaguely aware that it's been several seconds without me saying anything.

'Hi,' I say. Stupidly.

Kate smiles. Or maybe it's a sneer. Her clear blue eyes are as cold as a frosted windowpane in June. The kind that drips condensation on your sill and leaves your curtains with patches of mould.

'This is a surprise,' she says.

She hates me for what I did to Callum. She might as well wear a tee-shirt stating the fact.

I swallow. 'I came to see Cal.'

'Does he want to see you?'

God, she's terrifying. I feel my hands clamming up in my pockets. 'It's important,' I say. 'Please.'

She's a snide look away from a full-on eye roll. Sighing, she opens the door wider, giving me enough space to come in.

'I'll go see what Cal's up to,' she says. Her tone implies that I'm not invited to come with her.

Watching her go, I realise it's weird that Kate is here. How old is she now — twenty-two? Shouldn't she be in a dank mouldy flat somewhere in Dunedin, living the typical student life? What's she doing now?

As I wait in the entryway, I see that the Rigs' house hasn't changed at all. Its familiarity is like a salve to my cold encounter with Kate. I almost relax.

Which is when Callum's mum walks in.

Diana looks nothing like Callum or Kate: black curls, dark eyes, thick lashes. Her smile is warm but weary. I suppose the last three years haven't been kind to her. I wonder how much of that's my fault.

'Oh,' Diana says. 'Hello, Zelle. It's nice to see you again.'

She stands a good distance away from me, her arms lightly folded. Guarded.

'Hi, Diana,' I say.

She smiles again at the mention of her name. It doesn't quite reach her eyes. 'How are you?' she says.

'I'm good. How . . . how are you?'

'Good. Really good. I see you're working in Nicky's shop.'

I drag my shoe along the carpet, drawing a semi-circle with the toe of my boot. 'I am, yeah.'

'How's your mum?'

'She's good,' I say.

Diana stares at me a moment, maybe sussing me out in her therapist way. I avert my eyes.

It's starting to get awkward, but then there's the soft thud of footsteps on carpet, and Diana and I both turn to look as Callum ghosts in the doorway.

'Sorry,' I say to Diana, and practically sprint down the hall.

Callum's already back in his room when I walk in. I shut the door behind me before he has to ask.

And, Jesus, he looks like shit.

Roadkill-on-the-highway kind of shit. His hair is lank, his eyes are dull, and there are shadows under his eyes as if he hasn't slept in a week. I feel sick with guilt.

'Your room's just the same,' I say. I know I should be starting with the apology I've been rehearsing in my head all afternoon, but my throat is choked up and the words won't come out. Cal's room is as meticulously tidy as it's always been: not a single thing out of place. It's both comforting and unnerving to see how little it's changed.

Cal doesn't look at me. He takes his glasses off and wipes the lenses with the sleeve of his hoodie as if I'm not even there.

'What's Kate doing here?' I ask. 'Doesn't she live in Dunedin?'

Callum squints up at me. His eyes look so small without his glasses. His face seems naked. 'She did. Did her Master's, too. But she broke up with her boyfriend she was living with, so now she's back here for the time being.' Glasses now clean, he puts them back on. 'But you didn't come here to talk about Kate.'

I've got no choice now. I shift from foot to foot,

wondering if it's too late to run. It would make me the lamest, shittiest person to ever exist, but right now being the lamest, shittiest person feels like the most ideal option. Why are the most important things always the hardest to say? Why can't our friendship just be *easy* again?

'I'm sorry,' I say.

Callum just glares.

'I didn't *mean* to say it,' I scramble, realising that he's not going to fill in the silence for me. 'I was just upset and stressed and I wasn't thinking. I was mad, I guess, at the way Mac and Fox were treating me, so I just . . . blew. It was stupid. I'm sorry.'

Callum looks out the window. His bedroom has a view of the back garden. Descartes is on the grass, watching as a monarch butterfly swoops right over his head. He throws up a limp paw to try catch it, but promptly puts it down again, knowing his hunting days are far behind him.

'It was impulsive,' he says.

'Of course,' I say. 'I couldn't help it.' I hold my hands up in a plea. 'Really, Callum. You know I wouldn't have said it on purpose.'

'Really?' he says. His voice is too quiet, too steady. 'That's always how it's been with you, isn't it, Zelle?'

'Cal?' I can feel my jaw begin to quiver.

'You never mean to do it,' he continues. 'But you still do it anyway.'

'Callum, c'mon.'

He's gone even icier than Kate was at the door. I've never seen him so curt before, so callous.

'Fox and Mac told me I shouldn't have bothered reaching out to you,' he says. 'They said it wouldn't be worth it. I didn't believe them. I thought maybe you'd be better.'

I try to hold in the sob growing in my chest, but I crack, and let out a whimper that only makes Callum look more irritated. I blink to stop the tears from falling. 'Please,' I say. 'You're my best friend. I've never wanted to hurt you.'

He bites his lip. 'If that were true . . .' he says, then stops. 'If that were true, then you wouldn't have disappeared the day after Eli died.' He glares at me. 'I heard nothing from you. I only found out where you'd gone when my mum called your mum to ask where you were. You didn't even tell me you were leaving for Wellington. You didn't come to Eli's funeral. You didn't even call me to see how I was. You didn't fucking talk to me for three years.'

'It was complicated—' I say, but Cal cuts me off.

'And then you came back when it suited you, and you told everyone the secret I never wanted anyone to know. You knew better. That's not making mistakes, Zelle. That's just being a shitty friend.'

'And I don't want to be like that anymore,' I say. 'I'm here now. I can make things right.'

'But you're three years too late,' Cal says. 'You're too late, and I don't want to hear it anymore.'

I'm seconds away from falling on to my knees. 'What does this mean? What do you want?'

'It means I want you to get out,' Callum says. He doesn't shout; he doesn't even sound angry. And that makes it all the more awful. 'I mean it, Zelle. Get out and don't come back. Don't talk to me ever again.'

I don't have the strength to argue. I can tell from his voice that he means it, and that there's nothing I can do.

I don't say goodbye. I walk out, closing the bedroom door softly behind me. The tears spill over and I scramble to wipe them away, scared of running into Kate or Diana. But the house is surprisingly quiet. I stand in the hallway, spin a slow circle, but no one comes. I'm alone.

And I know as I leave the house that I'll probably never be back.

CALLUM

My Tim Cooney article is due in this week.

Given the mess of the last couple of days, it's fair to say that it's all but slipped my mind. Besides, ever since my interview flop, I haven't felt much motivation to write. Working for the *Stakesville Chronicle* feels pointless now that I know it hasn't got me anywhere. Like someone gearing up for a talent show while ignoring the fact they can't sing and never will, my life's dream seems doomed.

Still, when Keri, my editor, calls me early Saturday evening, I'm reminded that I'm contractually and morally required to produce a thousand words and have a deadline to meet.

'Do you know what day it is?' she says.

'Uh . . . It's Saturday?'

'Correct. And what does that mean?'

I glance at my calendar, searching for whatever it is that

I've obviously forgotten, but I have nothing noted for this Saturday. 'I don't know?'

'It's deadline day. Your interview with Tim Cooney was due in today, mate. Have you finished it?'

Fuck.

'Sorry?'

(Did I just swear out loud?)

'Nothing,' I gabble. 'I actually, um, I haven't . . . because of other things I've had going on, I—'

'Get to the point, Cal.'

'I haven't finished it.'

'You haven't finished it?'

'No. Well. It's almost done. Basically. I've got the whole thing transcribed, and I've drafted the article, but I still need to edit it, and proofread it, and check it over. So, it's done. It's just . . . not ready.'

'It's done but not ready, you say.'

'Yeah.'

'It's not like you to be behind on a deadline.'

'I'm sorry. I've had a rough week. I kind of forgot.'

I know it's vague and pathetic, but that's the struggle of living somewhere like Mistakesville. You can't make up an excuse that you've been on holiday or your grandma died or you had to take your dog to the vet, because everyone knows when you're on holiday and who your grandma is and that you don't have a dog. There are no secrets in a small town.

'Well,' Keri says, 'this is the first time you've ever been late for a deadline, so I can't be mad. You can have until tomorrow morning, all right? But then it's going straight to print. You'll have to oversee that. I'm away tomorrow evening to pick up my sister from Queenstown. She's flying in from Brisbane.'

Our deadline day is Saturday, so that Keri can lay everything out and do a final once-over to make sure everything's okay. Then Sunday night is what she calls our 'printing party', which basically means our five-strong team gather in our stingy office while we drink tea and print out a couple of hundred copies of the paper. Then early on Monday morning the *Stakesville Chronicle* gets distributed to all our newsstands (the café, the supermarket, the information centre, the medical centre, the retirement village, Nicky's Knick Knacks and the library), and gets picked up by anyone curious about the various shades of nothingness that happen here.

'Of course,' I say. 'Fine by me.'

'Amazing,' she says. 'Thank you, Callum. I trust you to get it polished off ASAP.'

'Yes, Keri.'

'Tim Cooney's great, isn't he? Such a kind, friendly person. Very passionate about this community.'

I suppress the urge to gag. 'He's certainly charismatic,' I offer.

'I hope he gets a second term.'

'It'll be exciting to see,' I say. 'Speaking of. I'll finish my article now. Bye, Keri.'

'See you later, Callum.'

I hang up. Lightly bang my head against the table.

Then I finish my article.

I open up my documents and re-read my first draft. Obviously, I can't hand this version in, so I create a new document and copy-paste the draft without the final two paragraphs. I replace it with a spiel about Tim Cooney's bullshit community involvement and a bland paragraph about the council and local government elections in general.

It takes me forever. Most of the time writing comes easily; I don't even have to think about it. It's like the words are already inside me, nearly perfectly formed, and all I have to do is let my fingers slide across the keyboard and give in to the flow. But casting Tim Cooney in a positive light sucks every ounce of writing joy out of me. The new draft is stiff and unnatural, but I know I have to do it. I plod on. When I finally feel satisfied enough with my work, the sun has disappeared, the air has cooled, and Kate's on the other side of my door calling me for dinner.

'Be there in a minute,' I call, emailing my article to Matt, who does the layout of the paper, then closing my laptop lid with a thunk.

But Kate, being Kate, waltzes into my room anyway.

'What are you doing?' she says. 'You've been locked up here all day.'

'Work.'

'Tim Cooney interview?'

'Yep.'

'Finished it?' She sits on top of my desk, swinging her legs.

'Yeah,' I say. 'Finally.'

'Why'd Zelle come over today?'

I look up at her. 'We had a talk. About the past. About Eli.'

'And what happened?' she asks, not in her demanding Kate way, but gently enough so that I know she's not pushing me for an answer.

'I don't think we're friends anymore,' I say, and even though I'd assumed that's what she wanted to hear, she still looks shocked.

'Oh,' she says. 'Wow. How do you feel about that?'

I look away. It's dark out, and the distant hills are barely more than lines and shapes and silhouettes.

'I miss Eli,' I say. I don't dare look at her. 'Please don't go soft, Kate.'

'I won't,' she says. 'I miss him too.'

Down the hallway, Mum shouts, '*Callum! Kate!*'

'Coming!' we call in sync.

And we get up and head for the kitchen as if we hadn't mentioned Eli at all. And that's the way I want it to be. See, the reason I don't want sympathy from Mum and Kate is not because I'm worried it'll make me sadder or make me cry (because it will, of course). I don't want their sympathy because as much as I miss Eli, I'm angry at him. And I feel like the worst person in the world for feeling that, so when it comes to Eli, I try my hardest to feel nothing at all.

Because before he died, he broke my heart.

Before Zelle ruined me, he ruined me first.

ZELLE

At school the Monday after Joe Rooney's party, it hits me: without Cal, I officially have no friends.

When I walk into Mr Abassi's classroom that morning, no one in the group will meet my eye. Everyone else is staring at me like there's a prize for it – they all know what went down at the party, and news of Cal and Eli's relationship has spread through the school like wildfire. As I make my way to a seat at the back, I feel just like I did at the party: isolated, locked out, like a mime trapped in a glass box.

That's how the rest of the day goes. And most of the next.

Until, that is, I'm called into Mr Appleby's office again.

'Oh, *come on,*' I mutter as Mr Harrington hands me the dreaded yellow note. Like the cruellest form of déjà vu.

Still, it's not like I have anywhere better to be.

'Zelle,' Mr Appleby announces, holding his door wide open. 'Welcome back. I'm glad you came.'

What I think he means is, *I'm surprised you showed up*.

He falls into his spinning office chair, and, reflexively, I find myself falling onto the sofa opposite him. He's slouched with one ankle crossed over the other and his hands holding onto his trousered shin. He looks relaxed, informal, but it doesn't ease the tension in my jaw.

'I'd like to begin with an apology,' he says. 'I'm sorry that I upset you last week. I know we got off on the wrong foot. So I'm proposing we try again. Make a fresh start. We don't have to talk about last week, or anything related to it. How does that sound?'

I shrug. I refuse to let him off easily. But his gentle smile tricks me into thinking that maybe I can trust him, so I soften my guard. Just a little. 'I don't care.'

'All right then.' He grabs a notebook and a pen from his desk, and rests them on his lap. I can see that my name is scribbled on a blank page in capital letters. 'I was thinking today we just have a chat. Get to know each other better. Would you mind if I took notes?'

'Why? Are you going to report back to my mother or something?'

'No,' he says. 'Here we're bound by confidentiality. In this room you can say anything you like, and I won't tell anyone unless, of course, I think you're in danger of hurting yourself or others. This is just for my personal record. The older I get, the harder it is to remember.' He laughs. 'Anyway. Am I okay to write some stuff down?'

I kick at the carpet with my shoe. 'I suppose if it's for your dementia diary,' I say, and to my surprise he laughs. It seems genuine. My mother would have yelled at me for saying that.

'How's school going?' he asks.

'It's okay. School's school.'

'Do you like your classes?'

'They're fine.'

'And what about friends?'

I decide to tell the truth on that one. 'I don't have any,' I say, which makes him raise his eyebrows ever so slightly. 'Not here, at least.'

He scribbles something in the notebook.

'What are you writing?' I ask.

He holds up the page to show me. In his distinctive all-caps scrawl, he's written, *NO FRIENDS???*

'Do you have people you talk to?' he says. 'People to sit with in classes? People to hang out with at lunchtime?'

'No.'

'Are there people you *could* talk to?'

'No.'

Mr Appleby taps his pen against his lip. 'There must be people here you were friends with before,' he says.

'Yeah, well,' I say. 'We're not friends anymore.'

Mr Appleby is quiet as he studies me. I can hear birds singing outside.

'I thought I *had* a friend,' I say, surprising myself. Maybe it's the loneliness getting to me, but after a day and a bit in almost complete silence, talking feels like a release.

Even if that means talking to the world's biggest dipshit of a counsellor. 'Callum. We used to be best friends. Before I left.'

Mr Appleby nods. Of course he knows Callum. He knows everyone at this school.

CALLUM, he writes.

'But I screwed things up,' I say. 'And when I came back here, I thought maybe I could make it better. But I just screwed things up even more.'

'Sounds complicated.'

'Yeah,' I say. 'It *is* complicated.'

I watch as he draws an arrow next to Callum's name, and writes, in smaller letters, *COMPLICATED*.

'What made you two friends in the first place?' he asks, like he's genuinely curious.

And despite everything, a smile breaks out on my face when I think about Callum and how good we used to be.

'Cal's great,' I say. 'He's so . . . simple. Easy-going. Calm. Even when we were kids. We were so opposite, and we fitted together perfectly.'

Mr Appleby smiles. A *keep talking* smile.

'And then . . . I don't know. Things changed. We stopped being so close.'

'Did something trigger that?'

I pretend to think about it, even though the answer's staring me straight in the face. 'It started when we were thirteen, just turning fourteen. Cal had his own stuff going on. Stuff that I wasn't a part of. We'd shared everything for years, and now he wasn't telling me anything.'

Mr Appleby writes *AGE 13/14 = DRIFTED APART*.

'And that impacted greatly on your friendship?'

'Yeah,' I say. But what I don't mention, of course, is that I wasn't telling Callum anything either. Mum and Dad had started fighting all the time, until they weren't talking to each other at all. At that point, Dad was already sleeping with the young German backpacker he'd eventually whisk off back to Berlin, though of course I didn't know that yet. How he managed to carry out an affair in a place as small as Stakesville would almost be impressive if it weren't so messed up. I'd try get out of the house as much as possible, and I relied on Callum to be my safety net. But not even his life was stable anymore. I had nowhere to turn. It was like we no longer trusted each other. We knew we were both keeping secrets from each other, but neither of us mentioned it.

'And did it escalate from there?'

'We started fighting a lot. Getting prickly with each other. There was a lot of tension between us.'

Despite that, I was staying at his house more and more often. Callum was asking more and more questions, and I wasn't answering them.

Mr Appleby writes down *TENSION*.

'Then what?' he says.

'And then we had our big fight. He told me he didn't want to be friends. And then our friend died and I moved to Wellington and I didn't talk to Callum again until I came back.'

Mr Appleby lets the silence drag. Whether he's quiet

because he's shocked or contemplative, I can't tell. 'That sounds like a lot, Zelle.'

'Yeah,' I say. 'It was.'

'I'm very sorry to hear about your friend.'

'Yeah.'

'Would you want to talk about them, too?'

'His name was Eli,' I say, remembering that Mr Appleby joined the school after I left, that he doesn't know about Eli. 'He was our friend, but he and Cal became pretty close towards the end.' I don't add that they were dating. I've already leaked that to our entire year group, and keeping it secret now is the least I owe Callum. 'He drowned in the lake.'

'I'm sorry that happened, Zelle,' he says. 'It must have been terrible.'

'It's okay.'

Neither of us speaks for a time.

'Three years is a long time without contact,' Mr Appleby says at last. 'What was that like? Seeing Callum again after all that time?'

'I thought it would feel like nothing had changed,' I admit. 'But when I finally saw him, I realised everything had. He's a completely different person now.' *And I'm not,* I think but don't say. Because the truth is, while Cal's grown, I feel no different from the person I was at fourteen. I might've moved away, but I've stagnated.

Which is a hell of a depressing thought.

'You said that you screwed things up with Callum again,' Mr Appleby says. 'What happened this time?'

I gaze over his shoulder while I try to think of what to say. There are inspirational quotes plastered to the wall. One of them says, *The best view comes after the hardest climb.*

Shoot me now.

'I . . . I broke his trust,' I say. 'I let him down. Again.'

Mr Appleby nods, and meets my eye with what looks like genuine sympathy. He must be a well-rehearsed actor. In the notebook he goes, *TRUST — BROKEN*.

'Do you think it's something you can work through?' he says.

'I don't know. I don't think I deserve forgiveness, anyway.'

Strangely, Mr Appleby's expression is unreadable. He studies me but says nothing; maybe he doesn't know what to say either.

'Well,' he says, finally. 'It appears that Callum means a lot to you.'

I nod.

'In my experience, a true friendship will always be salvageable. Even the most complicated ones.' He smiles. 'But now it looks like we've run out of time, Zelle. You'd best be off back to class.' He stands to walk me to the door. 'Will I be seeing you next week?'

'Maybe,' I say. 'If I feel like it.'

He grins. 'I'm hoping that's a yes. And Zelle?'

'Yeah?'

'I hope you and Callum sort it out.'

I give him a half-smile. Almost. 'Thanks,' I say.

I wish I believed it might be possible.

CALLUM

Something is very, very wrong.

And it starts with a text from Mum at 9.15 during first-period maths.

Have you read the latest issue of the Stakesville Chronicle?

I don't see the message until after class has finished and I'm on my way to media studies.

No? I reply.

Mum knows I don't usually read what I've written once I've sent it off. Even when I'm happy with what I've written, my perpetually perfectionist brain will always find some new flaw with it. The best way to deal with publication is to forget about it. Mum knows this about me.

Still, when she doesn't reply, I don't follow it up. Surely it can wait till I get home?

But then I get a text from Kate in the middle of media studies class.

CALLUM. What the HELL have you done?!?!?!

My heart picks up speed, just a bit. *What are you talking about?????*

Your Tim Cooney article!!!

What????? What about it?

typing …

typing …

KATE

THE FACT YOU JUST CANCELLED THE LOCAL COUNCILLOR?!

I drop my phone onto the desk with a clatter.

'Phone away, Callum,' Miss Nielsen says.

I wait until her attention shifts, then hide my phone under my desk.

What????? I type. *What do you mean???*

Oh God, I think. Oh God no. No. No.

'Callum,' Miss Nielsen says, casting a shadow over my desk. 'If you're not able to focus, give the phone to me.' She holds out her palm.

'Miss, I—'

'Morning break's in fifteen minutes,' she says. 'You can use your phone then.'

She wriggles her fingers.

I give her my phone.

Fuck, I scribble on my paper, where I'm supposed to be writing a practice essay on the New Zealand news industry. *fuck shit fuck fuck fuck.*

I really, really hope this isn't what I think it is. I think back to emailing my finished article to Matt. My impatience to get it done, Kate calling me for dinner, my brain still stewing over Zelle. Did I even check the document name? Had I made sure to send the right copy?

It's the longest fifteen minutes of my life before class ends.

'Be ready to concentrate next time,' Miss Nielsen says as she hands back my phone. 'Exams are coming up. It's an important time of year.'

'Thankyousorrythanks,' I mumble, and sprint out of the classroom.

I read Kate's latest texts.

'Such a statement is a blatant display of homophobia. Tim Cooney's disgust at a community simply embracing who they are is obvious' CALLUM YOU JUST CALLED OUT MISTAKESVILLE'S FAVOURITE PERSON AS A HOMOPHOBIC PRICK

YOU'RE CREATING A SHITSTORM

HOW DID KERI LET THIS THROUGH???????

IT'S FUCKING AMAZING, BTW. WELL DONE

Oh, God.

Shit.

Fuck.

Shit.

Mac, Fox and Finn are in the usual place under the tree.

'I need to get a copy of the *Stakesville Chronicle*,' I gasp. 'Right now!'

'Cal,' Fox says, 'are you okay?'

'Let's go. The supermarket will have some.' I'm breathing heavily like I've just run a marathon.

'We have to be back to class in fifteen minutes,' Fox says, but then he looks to Finn, and then to Mac, and stands up. 'All right. If we run it'll only take us five.'

And, without another word, we take off.

I lead the way, with Mac behind me, then Fox and Finn following in single file. We must look like prize idiots, charging along with our bags thumping on our backs. Mac runs a little faster until we're neck and neck.

'What's up?' she huffs between breaths. 'Is something wrong?'

'Explain later,' I puff. 'Not right now.'

Outside the supermarket, Mac takes charge. 'Take that seat over there,' she says, pointing to the bench that's set across the road in the Stakesville Memorial Garden. (What's it a memorial for? No one knows. The paint on the sign wore off years ago.) 'I'll go in.'

Obediently, we do. Five minutes later, she emerges holding a chocolate bar and a copy of the *Chronicle*. She darts across the street to join us, throwing the chocolate bar to me. 'Eat it,' she says. 'For your nerves.'

I bite off a square, even though my stomach feels too fluttery to digest anything.

'Okay, so what are we looking for?' she says, flipping open the paper.

I hold a hand over my mouth. 'My interview. With Tim Cooney.'

'The wanker guy?' Finn says.

'I always thought he was off,' Fox says. 'Mum thinks

he's great, though.'

'Found it.' Mac stabs her finger against the page.

'Read it,' I say.

'*Stakesville's Main Man: An Interview with Tim Cooney—*'

'Not out loud,' I say.

She goes quiet.

Fox and Finn lean over her shoulders, and the three of them start to read.

I force myself to watch them. Mac's face turns from calm, to confused, then shocked, and she looks up from the paper. 'Holy shit, Cal,' she says.

'*They should have the freedom to do as they please, but there's no need to show off about it,*' Finn recites, his voice climbing higher with disgust. 'God, what a prick.'

'*A councillor who wishes to deny the freedom of a long-oppressed group is long stuck in the past,*' Fox reads. '*Homophobia and ignorant privilege are not what the Central Otago Regional Council needs*. Fucking hell, Callum, I didn't know you could be this brutal.'

'This is great,' Mac says. 'Expose the hell out of him. Take him down.' She looks up at me. 'Why are you freaking out, Cal?'

'Because it was an accident! I sent in the wrong draft. That's not meant to be in there. I was supposed to write an *interview*, not an exposé.'

'But it's brilliant,' Finn says. 'Besides, Keri wouldn't have published it if she didn't think it was acceptable, would she?'

'She hasn't read it,' I say. 'I was late handing it in, so

Keri trusted me to proof it on my own. She *trusted* me to produce a quality piece, not a smear campaign.'

'Well. Shit.' Mac says. 'I suppose that makes it a bit more complicated, doesn't it?'

'I'm going to get in so much trouble,' I say.

Fox leans back on the bench. 'Suppose it is pretty controversial,' he says mildly. 'I mean, it's all true. And one hundred percent deserved. But Mistakesville's conservative. A lot of people won't be happy with this.'

'The *Stakesville Chronicle*'s not really intended for political slander,' Mac agrees. 'Or anything political, really.'

Just then my phone buzzes. It's a text from Keri.

Callum, meet me at the office after school today. Let's have a talk.

'Oh, God,' I say. I show my screen to the others. 'I'm going to get fired for this.'

'Nah,' Finn says. 'Surely not. Not if you say it was a mistake. And, anyway, I think it's a good thing. Starting a conversation that needs to be had. Giving criticism where criticism's due.'

'You don't know Keri,' I say.

'Keri is pretty terrifying,' Fox seconds.

Finn's face drops. 'Right. That's tricky, then.'

'We should get back to school,' I say. 'We're late.'

'Shit, yeah.' Mac stands, but none of us are in any rush to go. She drapes an arm around me. 'Are you sure you're okay to go back, Cal? You're not going to, like, have a stress-induced heart attack or anything?'

'I'm fine,' I say, which is a lie, and everyone knows it.

'Don't worry,' Fox says. 'This'll all blow over. In a week from now, everyone will have forgotten all about your article.'

'Yeah,' Mac says. 'Stand your ground. Explain the situation to Keri. What's the worst that could happen?'

'Don't make me answer that,' I mutter.

ZELLE

The rest of the school day, after my meeting with Mr Appleby, goes smoothly. I sit quietly in every class, avoid the Famous Five when I see them, and keep my head down during lessons. Mum picks me up at the end of the day. She's still mad about me sneaking out on Friday night, and when I hop into the car she greets me with a stiff hello. I can tell that something else is bothering her, though.

I can't help myself. 'What's wrong?' I ask.

'Nothing,' she says quickly, pulling out onto the street. She runs her teeth over her lip. It takes her a minute before she speaks. 'Walter emailed.'

There's a kick in my chest that feels like a football boot to the shin. My forehead feels tight. 'Why? What does he want?'

'I emailed him first,' Mum says. 'A couple of weeks ago. To let him know we were back at The Sanctuary. We need to think about our next steps, and the property is under his name, so . . . I'm calling him at nine tonight. To discuss things.'

I sit with this for a while, chiding myself for not thinking about this before — Mum and Dad aren't legally divorced, and Dad's the one who bought The Sanctuary, so ultimately all the decisions are up to him.

I feel Mum glance at me from the corner of her eye.

'You ought to speak to him too, Giselle.'

I let out a sarcastic huff. 'It's not like he cares what I have to say.'

'He's still your father.'

'Does he even count?'

Mum doesn't answer that. She turns up our driveway, slowing right down on the gravel. The BMW isn't designed for unsealed roads.

She places a hand on my knee. Her fingers stroke my corduroys.

'*Liefje,*' she says, and nothing more.

Inside I hole myself up in my room. Mum holes herself up in hers, and from the way Joni Mitchell is blasting I can tell she doesn't want to be disturbed.

At seven o'clock my stomach is growling and Mum still hasn't emerged. I look in the fridge, where there's a sad-looking carrot, a block of mince on the verge of expiry, and some cheese. I put salted water on to boil and heat olive oil in a fry pan. I dice an onion and some garlic, and grate the manky carrot, adding it in with the mince. I find a tin of tomatoes and some dried herbs in the pantry and add them in too. When the water boils, I drop in a handful of spaghetti. It's not *MasterChef*, but it'll do.

I knock on Mum's door, holding two steaming plates of pasta. She doesn't hear me, so I knock louder.

'Mum?'

'*Ja*?'

I open the door with my hip. Joni gets turned off. 'I made food,' I say, gingerly holding up the two plates. 'If you're hungry.'

'God, what time is it?' Mum puts her paintbrush down on the drop sheet. Her clothes are drenched with splatters of paint.

'It's seven-thirty.'

'Jesus.' She stands up and takes the bowl from me. 'Sorry. I lost track of time.' She sits down on the bed and begins to eat. I perch on the chair set up by her easel. We're not dinner-table people. 'Thank you for cooking, Zelle,' she says. 'That was kind of you.'

I blush and don't say anything. I'm not used to praise.

'What are you painting?' I say, distracting myself by looking at Mum's work in progress. There's a landscape that looks like our hills, but it's made up of angry, abstract lines, bright red brushstrokes stabbing the scene like wounds. The closer I look, the less formed it seems — classic abstract style. The sky is unfinished, but there are test patches of stormy greys and blues against the white. It's not pretty to look at.

'Just experimenting,' Mum says, shrugging. 'It's been a while.'

'It's good.'

'Thank you.'

We finish eating in silence. I take our empty plates back to the kitchen and put them in the dishwasher. I go to my room and pick at my guitar. Passing the time until nine o'clock.

When I hear Mum's voice down the hallway, I drop my guitar and creep out of my room. I crouch outside her bedroom door, my ear against the wall.

'We'll renovate,' she's saying. Her voice is brittle, tight. 'And we'll sell later in the year — it depends what Zelle does after she graduates school.'

There's hushed talk about finances. The conversation drifts into German, and Mum's voice gets further away, like she's moving across the room. Barely a quarter of an hour later she opens the door and holds out her phone. I don't try to pretend I wasn't eavesdropping.

'Walter's on the line,' she says. 'Do you want to say hello?'

I take the phone without looking at her and hold it up to my ear. I slip back into my room, closing the door but leaving the light off. My curtains are open and the moon is full, casting milky light over the walls.

'Hello?' I say.

Dad's voice grumbles. 'Hello, Giselle.'

I grip the phone tighter.

'Anneke says you're back at The Sanctuary.'

'Yep.'

'Renovating, then selling.'

'That's right.'

'How's school?'

'It's good,' I say. A good parent, a caring parent, would ask me what I'm planning to do after school finishes – where I want to go, who I want to be. A good child would probably answer without being asked. But neither of those things is true, so we don't pretend they are.

'You okay for money?'

'Yep.'

'I'll transfer you a deposit for your birthday,' he says. 'November 8. Coming up soon.'

'Yep.'

'You'll be seventeen, is it?'

'Eighteen,' I say. 'I'll be eighteen, Dad.'

'Right. I see. I see.' He sighs, and the silence stretches. 'Well. I'll be off, Giselle. International calls are expensive. *Tschüss*.'

'*Tschüss*,' I say, and he hangs up.

I throw the phone onto the bed and lie back against my pillows. It's several minutes before Mum comes in.

'Finished?' she says.

I nod. 'What did he say?' I ask.

'He'll send a deposit for the renovation costs.'

'How's his life going?'

'*Ik weet het niet*. We didn't talk about that.'

'He doesn't give a shit about me,' I say.

I can feel Mum give me a hard look. I sit up. 'He didn't know how old I'm turning this year,' I say. 'He doesn't know his own daughter's age, Mum.'

Mum's shaking her head. 'I'm sorry for asking you to speak with him. I shouldn't make you, if you don't want to.'

I bite the inside of my cheek.

'Sometimes, I—' Mum hesitates. She flutters her arms, then drops them again at her sides. 'I wish I'd seen through him earlier. I wish I didn't wait. I wish I'd left first, so I could've taken you with me.'

She turns, making to walk out.

'Mum?'

She stops.

'I'm sorry I snuck out on Friday,' I say. 'And I'm sorry for what I said to you. About Dad leaving.' I take in a shaky breath. 'It's not your fault he's an arsehole.'

It hurts my heart to see how surprised she looks.

'I forgive you,' she says, which isn't the same as saying *it's okay*, but I'll take it. She smiles, fleetingly, before she leaves me alone in the dark.

CALLUM

'You're fired.'

Keri sits across from me, her arms folded. My arms are out in front of me, waving like I'm gesturing for surrender, which I have been for the past ten minutes.

'Please,' I say.

'Unacceptable. Absolutely unacceptable.'

Keri is about fifty, the height of a child, and has a thing for knitted sweaters in all seasons. Right now she's wearing a burnt-red number with snowflakes across the front. It looks like something out of a Christmas catalogue.

'I trusted you with writing an article of integrity,' she seethes. 'Not this piece of slander.'

'I told you, it was an accident.' I press my hands onto the table, but I feel too vulnerable, so I put them back up again. Safeguarding. 'I wouldn't have sent it if I knew it was the wrong piece. I didn't *intend* for this to be published.'

'That's why you should have checked!'

'Technically, proofing my own articles shouldn't be my job.'

Keri pauses, blinks. She pulls down the hem of her sweater.

'I'm really, really sorry,' I continue. 'Please understand it was an accident. I didn't mean it—'

'I don't care if you didn't mean it,' Keri says. 'It's too late, Callum. It's gone out there. Tim Cooney's already seen it. I've had an email from his office accusing us of defamation. What kind of message would it send if I let you off the hook?'

I shrug. 'That we don't stand for some old guy's bigotry?'

'You shouldn't have noted down what he said in the first place,' she spits. 'Not when he'd said it off the record. It's a breach of journalistic ethics. And the right of reply.'

'Do the people on the receiving end of his comments get a right of reply?'

'Get out of my office,' Keri bellows. 'I'm sorry, Callum. You're a promising worker. But you've crossed a line.'

'But—'

'No buts. My decision is final.'

'You can't just—'

'I don't want to discuss this any further.'

'This isn't—'

'GET OUT OF MY OFFICE, CALLUM RIG.' Keri's voice is a magnitude 8 on the Richter scale. The knick-knacks on her desk quaver; a ceramic cat falls on its side. She reaches out a pudgy hand, picks it up and sets it back upright. 'I've got some serious reputational damage to fix. And shut the door behind you when you leave.'

I close the door to Keri's office with shaking fingers. The light shines all wrong and nothing feels real. On autopilot, I head towards the bathroom. I lock myself in the cubicle, squeeze my eyes tight, then blink three times. Then I throw up in the toilet bowl.

Now it feels real. Too real.

I'm not sure how long I spend there. I kneel at the base of the bowl until I'm too familiar with the patterns of the floor tiles and my head starts to throb. Eventually, I stand up, wipe my mouth with toilet paper, flush. I unlock the cubicle and wash my hands in the sink, then my face. I scoop a handful of water into my mouth and run my damp hands through my hair. I study myself in the mirror. My eyes are red, and drops of water drip down my neck and pool at the cuff of my shirt.

'*Fuck*,' I say.

Then I walk home.

I'm just by our front gate and reaching in my backpack for my keys when I hesitate. Mum and Kate will be home. Cooking dinner together, probably, or watching TV. They'll ask me how the meeting went. I'll tell them I got fired. Mum will freak; Kate will tell me to take it to the Human Rights Commission or something. Just the thought of the inevitable conversation exhausts me.

I keep on walking.

Finn's house is at the end of our street, nestled right in the scoop of the cul-de-sac where the street turns back on itself towards the direction of our place. There's a respectable car parked in the carport in a less-than-respectable garden. The front feels more paddock than garden lawn, with tall grass that tickles my legs as I walk up to the frosted-glass front door. I stand outside it for a minute. I only know this is Finn's place because he told me the house number. What if I knock and his dad answers and it looks obvious that I've just spent half an hour at the base of a toilet bowl? What if he thinks I'm some kind of dropkick and slams the door on me? What if I knock and Finn's not even there? What if Finn answers and thinks I'm some kind of weirdo for turning up unannounced? What if my bloodshot eyes and mussed-up hair are enough of a turnoff for him never to want to have anything to do with me again?

Heart pounding, I knock. Too softly. Like a mouse rapping on glass. I take a deep breath and try again. The knock comes out too harsh, too urgent, like I'm the police about to deliver bad news. Oh, God. No wonder I got fired from the paper. I'm too incompetent to even knock on a door.

Through the glass I see a figure moving closer. I feel like throwing up again.

'*Act normal,*' I whisper.

The door swings open.

'Hello,' a man says. He's tall and sinewy, a build just like Finn's. He has dark-gold skin and rectangular glasses perched on the end of his nose; his voice is gentle and lilts with an accent. 'How can I help you?'

'I . . . um—' It appears I've forgotten how to speak. In a voice that comes out all forced and wrong I blurt, 'Is Finn here?'

'Speak of the devil,' a voice calls down the hallway, and Finn bounces to the front door. 'Dad, this is Callum. He's not going to murder us. I've told you about him.'

(He *what*?)

'Ah, Callum,' Finn's dad says, extending a hand. 'I'm Anwar. Nice to finally meet you. Come in.'

(*Finally*?)

I shake his hand while I step inside. The house is bright and smells like spice and warmth. I bend down to start unlacing my shoes.

'Would you like to stay for dinner?' Anwar says.

I'm one more shallow breath away from launching into a panic attack. 'Oh, I don't have to—'

'You do now,' Finn says. 'Come on. I'll show you my room. Let's go.'

I don't even get a chance to wave goodbye to Anwar before I'm marched down to Finn's room.

'Sorry about the mess,' he says, opening the door. 'Organisation isn't my strong suit.'

Mess feels like an understatement. *Bombsite* feels more accurate. There are clothes strewn on the carpet and cardboard boxes stacked in haphazard piles. The desk is cluttered with paper and books and random objects. The only place that's tidy is the bed, where Finn sits.

'So, what's up?' he says. He leans back on his hands. 'How'd the meeting with Keri go?'

'Great,' I say. I'm still standing. 'She fired me.'

'You're kidding.'

'I wish.'

'That doesn't seem fair.' He stands up again and starts to pace. 'Surely there's something you can do, right? You made a genuine mistake. It happens. She can't turf you out over one mistake, can she?'

'I broke journalistic ethics,' I say, shrugging. 'What Cooney said was off the record. I shouldn't have written it down. It wasn't intended for anyone to hear.'

'But you exposed him as a homophobic prick,' Finn says. 'That's a good thing. Kickarse investigative journalism.'

'Investigative journalism doesn't really have a place in the *Stakesville Chronicle*.'

'Have you told Fox and Mac?'

'Not yet.'

He's quiet for a moment, thoughtful. 'So, what now?' he says.

I shrug again. 'Guess I'm unemployed. And my journalism career is over.'

'Aw, Callum,' Finn says. 'That's not true. Fox and Mac said you applied for broadcasting school.'

'Yeah.'

'There's no reason why you wouldn't get in.'

'Maybe there is now.' If my interview wasn't bad enough, being fired from a local paper for breaching standards would definitely earn a red line through my name. I hold my hands out at my sides. 'My life is over.'

'That's a bit dramatic.'

'I want to bury myself in a hole.'

'How would you sustain yourself?'

'I don't know. With wild berries and birds?'

'What if the berries were poisonous?'

'Christ, Finn, you could at least indulge me in my plans,' I say, and he laughs, which lifts my heart. He steps forward, then, and wraps his arms around me. I rest my head on his shoulder. He rests his chin on the top of my head.

'Why is life so damn *complicated*?' I say. Even though, right now, everything feels a little bit simpler.

I'm not sure how it happens. It's like a page missing from a book where the next scene doesn't quite fit with the last. One minute Finn's arms are wrapped around me and my chin is buried against his neck, and the next our noses are pressed together and my head tilts to the left and his hands move from my back to my cheeks and we're kissing.

We kiss softly, slowly. My heart is fizzing. I haven't kissed anyone since Eli. Finn's lips are steady, assured. I fall into the rhythm of it, letting my pulse slow as I run my fingers through the back of his hair. All too quickly it ends. We hold each other the same way as before, as if the moment never happened.

'Sorry,' Finn says. 'Was that okay?'

'More than okay,' I say.

When I finally arrive home, after dark and stuffed full of amazing Iraqi food, I've almost forgotten about the whole *Stakesville Chronicle* fiasco. My skin is still fizzing from kissing Finn. My heart flutters every time I think about it (which is all the time, every moment since it happened). I'm giddy and terrified and excited in a way I haven't felt in years.

thanks for coming over, Finn texts when I'm barely through my own front door. *v sorry about the situation with the chronicle, but I'm gonna be selfish and say I had a good time with you anyway*

I'm grinning like a little kid on Christmas morning. My fingers hover over my keyboard, wondering what to reply.

'Hey,' Mum says. 'How was your meeting with Keri?'

'Not ideal,' I say. 'She fired me.'

'*What*?!' Kate screams, leaping from the couch. 'She can't do that.'

'She can, and she did.' I hope my tone conveys that, as far as I'm concerned, the conversation is over.

It's not, of course.

'And you didn't fight back? *Callum*.'

'Kate,' Mum chides.

'There's nothing I could have done,' I say, somewhere between a sigh and a yell.

'Well, you could have at least *tried*,' Kate snaps.

'Leave it, Kate,' Mum says. She steps forward and hugs me. 'I'm sorry, Cal. How do you feel about it?'

'I dunno,' I say. 'I don't really want to think about it.'

I let Mum hold on to me for a few seconds more, then I pull away and retreat to my room, mumbling something about going to bed early. I turn off the lights and bury myself under the covers to re-read Finn's messages. I replay the kiss in my head. The excitement has been blunted by the reminder of the *Chronicle* fiasco, and now that I'm alone I'm thinking about everything that could go wrong and what the hell am I doing and what does Finn even see in me and what if I got spinach between my teeth at dinner and embarrassed myself in front of him *and* Anwar and what if I was awkward in a way that wasn't cute or funny or endearing and—

I had a good time with u too, I type, and quickly close the tab. And then I open my messages with Eli.

I'm still mad at you for what you did, you know, I write. *And I'm super pissed off at you for dying, because it means I don't even get a chance to be angry at you.*

And that I'm never going to be able to forget about you.

And then I turn off my phone and go to sleep.

ZELLE

The next day, Callum is the talk of the school. Not for the reasons I expect, though. It has nothing to do with Eli or what happened at the party or what I said or anything to do with me.

I first hear about it during second-period biology. Jade Turner and Maisie Donaldson are gossiping at the bench across from me instead of completing the worksheet.

'I heard it was an accident,' Jade says. 'How the hell do you publish something like that by *accident*?'

Maisie laughs her hyena laugh. Her head shakes from her shoulders like a bobble doll. I'm half-expecting her neck to snap from the strain of it. It would give everyone a break from her grating chit-chat. 'Maybe Callum's a rainbow activist now. So it wasn't an *accident*.' She says *accident* with finger quotes. 'Timing works with the whole Eli revelation.'

I have no idea what they're talking about, but I send them a glare that makes them twitch in their seats and look down. Fuckwits. I draw a sunflower on my worksheet and drill my pencil in till it tears the paper. Publishing? I don't know what that could be about. I'm dying to know, obviously, but I'd rather be strangled than lose my braincells trying to ask Jade and Maisie about it. And it's not like I can message Callum about it either. My outcast status has destined me to a fate of being forever out of the loop.

Callum's name bounces through my classes and the hallways like a basketball. I'm walking between third period to fourth when I see the gang enter the main corridor. Everyone stops to stare, but Cal keeps his head down. Fox and Mac flank him like bodyguards, and Finn's lanky figure shadows them from behind. Mac notices me first and looks through me, like I'm invisible.

I turn around and take the long way to class.

At lunchtime I head into the library. It's Loserville in here, but it's quiet, and it's not like I have people in line itching to hang out with me. I slump into a seat in the far corner and nibble at my sandwich. There's a newspaper on the table in front of me. The *Stakesville Chronicle*. I pick it up. It's been left open on a centre spread, thick blocks of text broken up with a photo that looks like the most generic stock image available of a bald white man. My eyes skim over the text.

Stakesville's Main Man: An Interview with Tim Cooney

By Callum Rig

Hold on.

I keep reading. The article — Callum's article, Cal's words in the town paper — starts like any other family-friendly profile of someone famous enough to be profiled but not famous enough for anyone to really give a shit about. It's clear our local councillor isn't going to win the Nobel Peace Prize anytime soon, but he sounds decent enough. Then I get to the final paragraphs.

Cooney's love of community appears to come with caveats. His personal opinions on the LGBTQIA+ community do not reflect his warm embrace of the people. In reference to the rainbow community, Mr Cooney said that 'they should have the freedom to do as they please, but there's no need to . . . show off about it [or] stick it in everyone's faces.'

Such a statement is a blatant display of homophobia. Tim Cooney's disgust at a community simply embracing who they are is obvious. His disparaging remarks show closed-mindedness and prejudice, and his community-centred approach loses all meaning when he refuses to show acceptance, care or even basic respect to the LGBTQIA+ group. Stakesville needs a strong-willed and visionary councillor to lead us into the future. But a councillor who wishes to deny the freedom of a long-oppressed group is stuck in the past. Homophobia and ignorant privilege are not what the Central Otago Regional Council needs.

'Fuck me sideways,' I say, and several heads snap in my direction.

'*Shh,*' someone says.

'Shut up,' I say.

'So, you've found it,' a different voice says, and I look up to see Fox sitting at the table next to me.

'What are you doing here?' I say in a whisper-shout.

He lays his pen down on his open notebook and lifts an eyebrow. 'Sacrificing my lunch hour to study for my physics exam. What are *you* doing?'

'Sitting in the loser corner,' I say.

He shakes his head almost imperceptibly. 'You found the article,' he says.

I look down at the *Chronicle*. Callum's name jumps from the page like it's 3-D. 'I heard everyone talking about it,' I say. 'I had no idea what they meant.'

'Well, there's your answer.'

'It was published by mistake?'

'Yeah.'

'Shit,' I say. 'It's good though. It's really good.'

'It's great,' he says, 'but it's been controversial, obviously.' He shrugs.

I look back down at the paper. My fingers stroke the pages.

'I didn't even know he writes for the paper,' I say.

'Well, *wrote,*' Fox says, then seems to remember he's talking to me and stiffens. 'He got fired for it.'

'No way,' I say. 'That's bullshit.'

Fox shrugs. I can feel the barricade that's come up

between us, the wall of defence, like we're separated by a sheet of glass. 'The situation's crappy, obviously,' he says. 'Doesn't help that it's front-page news in the entire town. It'll blow over in a couple days, though. By next week no one will even remember it happened.'

'Is he okay?' I say. 'Callum, I mean.'

Fox gives me a long, hard look. 'I'm not going to be your middleman, Zelle.' He twists his pen in his hands. 'If you want to know how Cal's doing, ask him yourself.'

'He doesn't want to talk to me.'

'So don't. If there's one thing you can do, it's give him the space he wants.' He closes his notebook, pen marking his page. He stands up and grabs his bag from the ground. 'I'm meeting up with Mac to revise for our test. See you later, Zelle.'

'Bye,' I say, but he's already turned away and headed towards the exit. My goodbye hits empty air.

CALLUM

Kate bursts into my room at seven on Thursday morning.

'Cal! You've got to see this.'

I'm getting rather sick of surprises.

But Kate is either too preoccupied with her own enthusiasm to notice the lack of mine or is choosing to ignore it (probably the former), because she holds her phone in front of my face and squeals, 'It's about you!'

'Huh?' I prop myself up to sitting, reaching for my glasses. I take the phone from her outstretched hand and read what's on the screen.

Maybe it's the fact that I woke up about thirty seconds ago, but I don't think my eyes are reading quite right.

'Huh?' I say again.

'They're talking about you in the regional paper!' Kate says. The piece is titled *Boomer Backlash: Why I stand with the writer of the Tim Cooney controversy*. It's written by a senior editor at the *Central Star*, a Central Otago news outlet that's slightly more important than the *Stakesville Chronicle*.

The writer of the article praises me for my *bravery and honesty*, for *exposing ugly small-town truths*, and thinks that me being fired from the paper *is a tragedy in the fight for free speech. Journalistic ethics were broken*, the article continues, *but we should be championing Callum Rig for his sense of social justice, not punishing him for a mistake made by a promising talent not afraid to expose life's injustices.*

This must be a joke.

Please tell me it's a joke.

'This is a joke, right?'

Kate snatches her phone back. 'Course it's not a joke,' she says. 'This is great, Cal. This could get you back on the team for the *Chronicle*! Shit, maybe the *Central Star* will hire you! This could end up on the six o'clock news. You're famous!'

I fall back against my pillow. 'God, please, no.'

'What?' Kate says. 'This is a good thing, isn't it?'

I rub my hands over my face. 'I don't want to be famous, Kate. I just want this whole thing to be forgotten.'

'But this is your *career*, Cal. This is your *dream*.'

'How'd the *Star* even find out about this, anyway?'

'Through the statement on the *Chronicle*'s website, I'm guessing,' she says. 'You know, Keri saying, *I'm so sorry for the article, Callum Rig has been fired blah blah blah*—'

'I know the statement, Kate.'

'Well, I think you should be excited about this. You never know what might come out of it.'

'Nothing, I hope.' I pull the covers over my head. 'I'm going back to sleep.'

'I think Kate has a point,' Mac says. It's lunchtime, and she has the article up on her phone while Fox and Finn stand either side, peering at the screen. 'I understand that you want this to blow over, but this piece could be a good thing, you know. Might open up opportunities.'

'Yeah, like being the laughing stock of the whole school for the rest of the year,' I say. I fling my arms out like wings. 'No, the whole *town*. And now probably the entire region. This'll stick with me for the rest of my life. Haunting me. It'll probably end up in my obituary.'

'Suppose you could dig that hole for yourself after all,' Finn says, which is met with quizzical looks from Fox and Mac. The left side of Finn's lip curls up. Which reminds me of our kiss the other day, which reminds me of the fact that we haven't talked about that kiss since it happened apart from over Messenger and that I haven't been alone with Finn since it happened and oh my God I kissed *Finn* while my life is currently completely falling apart and everything is going wrong and the last thing I need is this goofy boy with his infectious smile to complicate things even further—

'You're catastrophising, Cal,' Fox says. I see the way his eyes dance from Finn to me (am I blushing?), then to Mac, and I see the look that passes between them and choose to ignore it. I steadfastly avoid Finn's eye.

'The school's full of idiots,' Fox continues. 'They're

giving you shit for this because they're bored. Even if it's not now, it'll blow over sometime soon. It has to. Something else mildly scandalous will feed the gossip chain and everyone'll forget this ever happened.'

'Where's Zelle when you need her?' Mac whispers.

Fox rolls his eyes at her.

I wring my hands at my sides.

'Cal,' Mac says. The three of them are still shoulder to shoulder. '*Relax*.'

'I wish.'

'Is it broadcasting school you're worried about?' Mac says. 'Because don't be. They shouldn't let this influence their decision. And if they do, they're stupid, and I'm staging a protest until they accept your application, and you can't stop me.'

The thought of getting accepted almost makes me laugh. I consider telling them the truth about the interview, but don't want their pity, so I plaster on a smile and say, 'Thanks.'

But, God, it hurts keeping so many secrets.

Finn finds me in the library during our study period.

'You hiding from me or from studying?' he says, flinging himself into the chair beside me. I sit up from where I've been dozing on the desk.

'Both,' I grumble.

'Exhausting day, huh?'

I rub at the tension headache that's building across my brow. 'I just want all this to go away.'

'I feel like I moved here at the wrong time,' he says. 'Or maybe the right time. I don't know. It's good drama.'

'Shut up.'

'I know you think I'm hilarious.'

I start to pull a face, but I can feel a grin breaking out instead. 'Want to go outside?' I say.

Finn jumps up.

We sit on the bench under the oak tree, the shadows of the leaves imprinted on our legs. It's quiet, awkward, but not a totally unpleasant kind of awkward.

'It was nice when you came for dinner,' Finn says.

'Yeah.'

'My dad likes you.'

'I barely said three words.'

'I think he appreciated the quiet.'

'Have you been with a guy before?'

He kicks a leaf with the toe of his shoe. 'Dated, yeah. Been in a relationship with, no. Have you—' He pauses. 'Been with anyone else? Other than Eli?'

'No.'

'Wow.'

'Yeah.'

'That's a long time.'

'Not exactly spoiled for choice here.'

'Thank God I came along.'

'S'pose you're adequate,' I say, and before I'd barely noticed how Finn's fingers had looped over mine, his hand slowly makes its way up my arm. My skin tingles and my pulse picks up and I lean forward and kiss him first—

And I get the sense that someone is watching us.

And I flicker open my eyes.

And I look right at Zelle.

ZELLE

There are two people kissing on the bench under the oak tree.

I roll my eyes because, well, *obviously*. At least wait until school is finished so the whole world doesn't have to watch. But of course I go closer to see who it is, because in this shithole place I'll take any kind of entertainment I can get, even if it's watching two horny teenagers get it on in the middle of the school field, and so I step forward and—

It's Callum.

It's Callum, kissing Finn.

Fuck me sideways.

My rubbernecking obviously isn't subtle enough, because Cal stops, and I don't have time to turn around and run before his eyes burst open and he's staring straight at me.

'Oh,' he says.

'*Shit.*' I hold my hands up. 'Fuck. Shit. Sorry. I didn't mean to stare. I was just walking past, and . . . sorry. This looks bad. Sorry. I'll go now.'

I run off with my cheeks flaming red. I'm not entirely surprised, because Cal with a crush is about as obvious as an elephant in a tutu trying to pass as a ballerina. I even consider texting him about it, before I remember his strict no-contact rule. A fresh ache washes over me. I don't get to tease Cal anymore, be his wingman, be the one he runs to with all his worries and hopes and mad overthinking. Not that I did a good job of that last time. Not that he even told me anything.

He corners me at my locker at the end of the day.

'What you saw today,' he says, without even saying hello. His mouth is set in a firm, hard line. 'With me and Finn. Don't tell anyone about that.'

'Of course not,' I say.

'I don't know what we're doing. We're just . . . messing around. So, don't spread it round the whole school, okay?'

'I won't,' I say. 'You can trust me, Cal.'

'Well, evidently I can't,' he says as he turns his back and walks away.

That's the most we talk for the entire week.

CALLUM

By the start of next week the *Chronicle* debacle has gone national.

When I see the link to the article Mac posts to the group chat, it seems like some kind of cosmic joke. Definitely a fever dream. Nightmare, more like. I click on the link.

It's real.

The opinion piece in the *Herald* talks about my interview, my getting fired, the article in the *Central Star*. I can't even read it all before I throw my phone onto the pillow and bury my head in my hands.

Finn, Fox and Mac wait outside my front door.

'Don't even mention it,' I say.

We don't talk about it.

Then my phone rings during media studies. This is embarrassing for two reasons: one, because the class is dead silent, and two, because everyone stares at me like

I've just told an inappropriate joke.

'Sorry,' I say. I'm about to decline the call, but it's from an unknown number, so my finger hesitates over the red reject button. I run out of the class. Miss Nielsen gives me the side-eye.

I answer on the final ring.

'Hello?' I say. I feel flustered: I hate phone calls at the best of times. I hate them even more in the middle of class, from numbers I don't know, for reasons I don't want to think about. A series of worst-case scenarios runs through my head. Kate's dead, Mum's dead, Anwar's calling to tell me to stay away from his son and that I'm not welcome at their house ever again.

'Is this Callum Rig?' a woman's voice says.

'Uh,' I say. 'Yeah?'

'My name is Jazz Ruwhiu. I'm the student leader at the broadcasting school's Politics in Media Club. Is now a good time to talk?'

What?

'What?' I say.

'Our group's noticed your recent publicity with the Tim Cooney article,' she continues. 'We think it's great, by the way. And it's opened up some pretty heated debate. Anyway, I did a Google search of your name, and I saw on the *Chronicle*'s Facebook page that you'd applied to broadcasting school, and I got your phone number from your Facebook account, so here we are.'

'My phone number's on my Facebook account?' I say.

'You might want to adjust your privacy settings.'

There are bricks in my stomach, in my head, in my increasingly sweaty hands. Where is this going? 'Right,' I say.

'As you might know, our open day is coming up in two weeks. The PMC – the Politics in Media Club, that is – are hosting a panel discussion over the weekend, on campus, where we talk about, you know, politics in media. So, since you're a hot topic at the moment, and I assumed you'd be going to the open day anyway, we'd love to have you on our panel. I know you're not officially a student here, but we attract a pretty big audience. It'll definitely look good for your application. So. Are you in?'

My head is reeling. I grip the phone tighter, trying to process Jazz's words, this conversation, this entire scenario. Me? In a panel discussion? In a *political* discussion?

'Oh, God,' I say.

'I can give you some time to think about it,' she says. 'But know that we'd love to have you. And this can definitely open some doors.'

I *am* thinking about it. In the swirling mess of my thoughts, I'm thinking about it. Being on a panel might not make up for my shitshow of an interview, but it could give me the edge I need. I can prove to the school that I'm worth it. I can redeem myself from getting fired, take back control, show the school, the industry, the world that I take this stuff seriously. This might be my last chance. And no one would ever have to know how close I came to it not happening.

But here's the problem. The big problem.

The broadcasting school's campus is in Wellington. Mum took me up for last year's open day, when I was still deciding on my options. Jazz seems to assume I'm already going to be there. Which I'm not. And no one knows about my disastrous first interview, which means no one can know about this.

I have to do this alone. In secret.

But how am I going to get to Wellington on my own?

'Callum? Are you still there?'

'I'll be there,' I say, the words flying from my mouth before I can stop them. 'I'll be at the open day. And on your panel.'

'Fantastic,' says Jazz, sounding surprised I've decided so quickly. 'That's fantastic, Callum, thank you so much. I'll grab your email, and I can send out some details about the when and where.'

I give her my email address, exchange thank yous and goodbyes, then hang up and slump down the wall until I'm sitting, head down, on the scratchy blue carpet outside the classroom door.

I need a plan.

I don't have a plan.

Not for the first time I feel royally, totally, absolutely screwed.

When I look up, I find I'm not alone.

There, standing at the other end of the corridor, is Zelle.

ZELLE

I'm so focused on walking back to Mr Harrington's biology class after my session with Mr Appleby, I almost don't notice the sandy-haired boy slumped at the end of the corridor. Probably just some kid who's been kicked out of class for running their mouth one too many times. But then the boy sighs, seismically loud, and I look more closely.

Only Callum knows how to sigh like the world is ending.

'Are you okay?' I say, before thinking about it. Would he really want me to ask that? Would he really want to tell me?

He answers my questions for me. 'What's it to you?'

I slump on the ground across from him. 'I know I'm a shitty person, but I'm not shitty enough that I'd walk past you sighing in despair and *not* ask you if you're okay.'

He looks away, his expression somewhere between soft and serious. 'I never said you were a shitty person,' he says quietly.

'Okay, okay, but this isn't about me,' I say. 'What's up with *you*?'

Cal looks at me as if I've just said something revelatory, which makes me feel both irritated and embarrassed. I'm expecting some sort of smart retort from him: *Since when is anything NOT about you? Why do you want to know, anyway? So you can have more secrets to spread about me?*

But, instead, he says, 'I'm screwed.'

He's talking to me? He's offering me information? I want to get up and skip down the corridor, but this conversation feels fragile, and I'm scared that making a big deal of it will slam shut this door that's creaked open between us. I pull my knees to my chest, and in my softest, most casual voice ask, 'Why?'

He takes off his glasses and rubs at his eyes. 'I signed up to join some political discussion panel,' he says. 'For the broadcasting school's open day. In Wellington.'

'And?' I say, not getting it. 'That's a cool thing, right? What's the problem?'

'The problem is that no one can know about it,' he says, and the words fall out of him. 'The thing is, I had my interview for broadcasting school a few weeks back. I screwed it up, but everyone thinks I did amazing, so this opportunity, it's like a second chance. It might get me accepted after all. But if people know it's my second chance, they'll know how close I came to not getting in.

And if I mess up this time, everyone will know that I screwed up twice. I can't let that happen. But, also, I don't know how I can get to Wellington by myself.'

'I'll come with you,' I say, without hesitation.

Callum looks at me like I've just pulled out a gun. 'What?'

'We've still got our apartment in the city,' I say. 'I've got the keys. And I've got enough money from working at Nicky's to buy plane tickets, and you'll have savings from working at the *Chronicle*, right? We can afford it, if we put our money together. We'll say we're going camping for the weekend, drive out to the airport and stay at mine. Easy.'

The idea's only just come to me, but already I see it blooming: finally, I can go back to Wellington. It's only for a weekend, but I can catch up with Anahera and Lucy and Tabitha, remind them I'm still their friend, that I haven't disappeared forever. And I can see Luka, show him that it was worth waiting for me, that we can—

'No,' Cal says, shaking his head. 'Definitely not.'

'It's not that bad,' I say, still lost in my daydreams about going back. Going *home*. 'It's not like we're doing something illegal or anything.'

Callum glares at me like I'm completely missing the point. 'I'm not going on a trip with the person who spilled my biggest secret to the whole school. Amongst other things.'

Oh, yeah.

I guess I am missing the point.

'Look,' I say, standing up, shifting away from the wall.

'I'm sorry, and I'm not going to stop being sorry, but I want to make things right with you, Cal. This is the least I can do for you. Think of it like redemption. Or compensation.'

But Callum's still shaking his head. He stands up too, giving himself space. 'Don't be silly, Zelle,' he says. 'You can't *do me a favour* and expect that's enough to make things okay. That's not how forgiveness works, and you know it.'

'What do you want me to do, then? What will it take for you to forgive me?' I say. My voice is raised.

Callum's is, too. 'Maybe I don't *want* to forgive you,' he says. 'Maybe I just want you to leave me alone, like I've asked you to, and stop messing with my life more than you already have.'

He's glaring. I'm glaring. The bell signalling the end of the period breaks the silence for us.

I lean in closer to him, slinging my bag over my shoulder. 'You need to go to Wellington,' I say, whispering now, 'and I can help you do that. I'm not searching for forgiveness. I'm not searching to fix things. I'm just offering to do this, for *you*.'

The classroom door bursts open and students flood the hallway like a river bursting its banks. I use the sudden din to spare Callum from giving me a response, and I walk away.

CALLUM

I am *not* going to Wellington with Zelle.

It'd be like going on holiday with the person who stabbed you to near-death and pretending that everything is fine and dandy. *Let's put past sins behind us, pledge forgiveness and be on our merry way as best friends.*

I can't think of anything worse.

I meant it, too, about not wanting to forgive Zelle. I just want her to leave me *alone*. Let me continue with my life, and leave me to pick up the pieces from the messes she's created.

ZELLE

It's like my conversation with Cal never happened.

The next day he's back to ignoring me as if I'm a ghost. I notice he's by himself more often, though, walking down the hallway between classes alone, not flanked by the rest of the Famous Five like he usually is. I'm getting the sense his separation is intentional, but it's not like I can ask.

Of course he'd say no to going with me to Wellington. It's a crazy idea, stupid. Somehow, though, I'm still half-expecting him to change his mind, so the longer he avoids my eye, the more my disappointment is like a rock at the bottom of my stomach. I want to do this for him, but it seems he doesn't want my help.

And there's nothing I can do about that.

CALLUM

A couple of days after my encounter with Zelle, Finn asks me if I want to come over after school.

'I have assignments to do,' I say. I'm not sure why I'm hesitant. But I am. Finn's smile is irresistible, though, and so is his eye roll.

'Callum Rig,' he says, 'isn't the point of being young to procrastinate on assignments and make bad decisions?'

'Do you know who you're talking to?'

He squeezes my shoulder. 'Think of this as exposure therapy,' he says as we continue past my house and down to the end of Smyth Street.

Anwar's not home – still at work, Finn says as he unlocks his front door – and I feel both anxious and relieved that we're alone. Without appearing even to give it a second thought, Finn strides into his bedroom and dumps his bag on the floor.

I follow, gingerly, and perch myself at the edge of his bed. He doesn't seem to notice my hesitation, because as soon as I'm sitting down, his hand cups my cheek, his other hand holds my waist, and we're kissing.

After a few moments of soft kissing, Finn breaks away and meets my eyes. His left hand is still latched onto my waist. I get the sense he's giving me breathing room; asking, without words, if I'm okay.

In answer, I pull his lips back to mine.

This time we kiss with urgency. His tongue slips into my mouth, and I find mine doing the same.

And while we kiss, I remember.

I remember being fourteen and home alone at Eli's house. It was December, school was almost over, and Eli and I were spending more time alone than we ever had before. I remember that too-hot afternoon, playing video games in the family media room, Eli dropping his controller at the end of a game and holding my gaze.

I said, 'Do you want to play another round?'

He said, 'Have you ever kissed anyone before?'

I turned away and blushed. 'No,' I said. 'Have you?'

He shook his head.

'Why are you asking?' I said.

He shrugged. 'Have you ever wanted to try?'

I dropped my controller in my lap. 'Yeah,' I said. 'I guess so.'

'We could try.'

I looked up.

'Like, now?'

'If you want,' he said. 'Just to try it.'

I pull away from Finn.

'Callum?' he says. 'Are you okay?'

I don't answer. Kissing him is mind-blowingly, heart-thrashingly better than okay.

But so was kissing Eli.

When Eli finally pulled his lips from mine, his eyes were still closed. I watched them flutter open, his brown eyes shining amber in the light, staring into my face in a way that no one had stared at me before.

'Let's keep this between us, okay?' he said.

'I should go,' I tell Finn.

He looks like I've just given him whiplash. 'You just got here.'

'I have stuff to do.'

'What's wrong?' he says.

I leap up from the bed. Tearing myself away from him hurts. But I remember the rush I felt when Eli asked to keep our secret between us, the rush at the idea of there being an *us*. That was the moment I started to pull away from Zelle, the moment I discovered what it was like to tell a secret to someone that wasn't her. It's not like she'd done anything to make me *not* want to tell her stuff. But with Eli, we'd just created something that was *ours,* and I was desperate for more.

And look where it got me.

I don't think I can bear that pain a second time.

'Nothing's wrong,' I say, but it comes out like an accusation.

Finn's not letting me go easy. 'You seem mad.'

'I'm not mad.'

'You're acting like it.'

'I'm not acting like anything.'

'You're acting like you have a problem with me.'

'Jesus, Finn, I don't have a problem with you!'

A knot forms in his brow. I simultaneously want to punch it and kiss it. 'Then why are you acting like you do?' he says.

'Because maybe I don't want this!' I say. 'Because maybe I just want to be friends.'

The knot in Finn's forehead has untangled to an expression that I can barely stand to look at. 'You don't want this,' he repeats. Like he can't get himself to absorb the meaning.

'No.' (*Stop,* my brain is telling me. But my body won't listen.)

He runs his hands through his hair. 'Why'd you never say?'

'Because you never asked.'

Finn looks down, biting his lip. When he looks back up at me, I can see he's trying hard not to cry. 'Is it because of Eli?' he says. 'Because—'

'No!' I say, and it feels like something in me snaps. 'And you don't know the first thing about me and Eli, so don't act like you do.'

I'm expecting him to fight back. Finn doesn't seem like a quitter. Instead, he lets out a sigh, like his whole body is deflating, and he sits back down on the bed.

'Okay,' he says. Then again, more to himself: 'Okay.' He runs his hands over the bedspread, smoothing out the creases. 'I'm sorry.'

'I'll see you later, Finn,' I say.

But he doesn't reply.

ZELLE

I'm alone in my room when my phone rings.

'Cal?'

His breathing is thick and heavy, and he sounds like he's been crying. 'Hey,' he says.

'Are you okay?'

'Fine,' he says, too quickly. 'Look . . . okay. I'll go to Wellington with you. You win.'

'Let's book some plane tickets, then,' I say.

Press Release from the Office of Councillor Tim Cooney

Last week, an article was published in the *Stakesville Chronicle* by writer Callum Rig that referenced disparaging remarks regarding the LGBT community I supposedly made during an interview. The nature of the interview is unprofessional and defamatory, and I am pleased to know that Mr Rig has been stood down from his position and all copies of this issue of the *Chronicle* removed from shelves. The online article has also been deleted.

These comments were taken out of context and framed purely to degrade my integrity as a local politician and spokesperson for Stakesville. I have the utmost respect for the LGBT community and for people of all genders and sexualities, and I am appalled by this act of political slander.

I will not let these lies deter me from my job, and I am proudly still running for the Stakesville ward at the upcoming local body elections.

CALLUM

The next day at school with Finn is weird.

He doesn't wait for me outside my house, and he barely talks to any of us when we meet up on the way to school. Fox and Mac must know something's up — Finn usually talks enough for all of us.

'Got plans for the weekend?' Fox says during lunch. 'We could do a study session at mine on Saturday. My parents are out, so we have free rein.'

'*Study session*,' Mac adds with finger quotes.

'Can't this weekend,' Finn says, not looking at us. 'I'm going to Alexandra. To see my mum.'

'I can't either,' I say. 'Kate's taking me to Queenstown.'

Mac looks at me with a quirked eyebrow, and Fox watches both of us with an expression somewhere between confusion and bewilderment. 'Well, never mind, then,' he says, waiting for an explanation that neither of us gives.

When Finn hurries off after our last-period class without waiting for us, it's clear the issue can't be ignored any longer.

'What's going on between you and Finn?' Fox pounces.

'Nothing,' I say, immediately defensive.

'Doesn't look like nothing.'

Mac is silent, but from the way she's chewing her lip I know she's brewing about something.

'Why do you assume it's a problem between us?' I say. 'Maybe he's just going through his own stuff.'

'Because he obviously isn't,' Fox says, and his tone surprises me. Fox is the mellow one, the peacekeeper of the group. He never gets angry. 'It's obvious the problem is about you. Hell, he barely made eye contact with you today. It's like he was pretending you didn't exist.' He pauses. 'You like each other, don't you? Are you seeing each other?'

'We *were*,' I snap, 'but it's not a big deal, and it's none of your business, so I don't know why you care so much.'

Fox holds my eyes for a long time. 'But it *is* our business, Cal,' he says, and dread fills my stomach as I realise these words sound like ones he's been rehearsing for a long time. Like this conversation was planned.

I look over at Mac, who's steadfastly avoiding my eye. She's staring at the ground, tearing off her lips with her teeth, but my heart drums harder when I hear her sniff and I notice, oh God, she's crying.

'Mac? What's going on?'

'*You!*' she explodes so suddenly I take a step back.

She points a finger at me. '*You,* Callum. You don't tell us anything. But do you ever think about how that makes us feel?' She wipes her eyes. 'Of course I think it's shitty what Zelle did at Joe's party. But I also think it's shitty that you never told us about Eli.'

'So *that's* what this is about?' I say, sparking with fury as I remember yesterday at Finn's house. 'You're mad that I have a life? That I'm not just Zelle's puppet and, God forbid, that I have my own secrets?'

'Eli was our friend too!' Mac says. 'We were the Famous Five for a reason, Cal. We were all friends. And it's not just you who's grieving, you know. We miss Eli, and you don't get to gatekeep him just because you were in love with him—'

'I wasn't in love with Eli!'

'—And Finn's our friend, too, in case you hadn't noticed. We're a *group,* Callum, and you don't get to block us out from what's going on with our own goddamn *friends,* not when it affects all of us.' Mac sniffs.

My eyes ping from her to Fox. 'So you've been talking about me?'

Fox nods. 'It hurt us, Cal,' he says. 'It hurt that you won't talk to us. We're the Famous Five.'

'The Famous Five died when Eli died,' I say, my throat tight, 'and when Zelle fucked off. It's dead. It's been dead for years. It probably never existed in the first place.' I walk between them. 'I have to go home.'

Except I don't.

I walk loops around the streets, trying not to think and failing miserably. A bone-chattering drizzle weeps from the sky, and I'm cold and stiff and exhausted but I don't want to go home. I end up on the cycle path on the outskirts of town. If I keep going, eventually I'll end up in Alexandra, then Queenstown, then over the Southern Alps, then into the Tasman Sea. Maybe I can start a new life in Australia, with better weather and proper malls.

There's a bald-headed man striding towards me, rain wicking off his fluorescent red jacket. I look down, because it's too intimidating to say hello to strangers, but I feel the man's eyes on me.

'Callum,' he says in a voice that sends a knife through my chest.

It's Tim Cooney.

Oh, God.

How do I get out of here?

'Don't run off,' Cooney says, and oh God, we're on a desolate trail on a rainy day and no one's around and the local councillor is about to kill me and I won't even be a martyr for the cause because I've made enemies out of all my friends, and Finn's right, I probably will be buried six feet under the ground to the soundtrack of Nickelback—

'Your article was extremely unprofessional,' Tim Cooney says. 'I'm not out here to make enemies, Callum, but proper journalism doesn't involve slander of your subject. I hope you know the impact this has had on me. This has been extremely tough on me, the council, my family—'

'I'm sorry,' I squeak.

'Count yourself lucky that you've been let off the hook like you have. Being fired from the paper is a pretty merciful punishment, you know. Other people would have sued for defamation.'

The drizzle continues, like even the clouds are on Cooney's side. And I have no idea why, but of all things I could and should be thinking about, it's Zelle's voice that echoes in my head. Zelle, her forehead fixed in her permanent pissed-off expression, rolling her eyes as she says, *Are you really going to take this shit, Cal?*

'You know what?' I say. 'I'm sorry for not proofing my article before it went to print. But I'm not sorry for what I said in it. I think the community you care so deeply about deserves to know what you really think about some of its members.'

(*Shut up*, a voice screams inside my head. *This is a terrible idea. Stop and run and get out of here alive.*)

But I don't move.

'You should *not* have recorded what I said—'

'And you should not have such horrible opinions about your fellow human beings,' I say. His mouth opens and closes, and I carry on before he has the chance to gather his words. 'Sorry,' I say, 'but I have to go. Nice to talk, Tim. And best of luck in the election.'

ZELLE

I barely sleep the night before we leave.

When my alarm goes off at six, I've already been awake for ages, watching the dawn seep through the curtains. Callum said he'd be here by seven. He wants to get to the airport early, 'just to be on the safe side'.

('We're flying to Wellington, Cal, not to the other side of the world. There's no need to get to the airport so early.'

'Are you coming with me or not, Zelle?')

And he calls *me* annoying.

I packed last night — a huge duffel bag way too big for a weekend trip, but still. I've taken advantage of the extra packing room and half my wardrobe is stuffed inside, including an outfit for going out tonight. It's my black sheath dress. Luka said I looked hot in it.

I sneak into the kitchen and quietly pour myself a bowl of cornflakes. As far as Mum knows, I'll be at work with

Nicky. As far as Nicky knows, I've called in sick with a stomach bug. I'll call Mum later to tell her not to pick me up because I'm having a sleepover at Mac's. She'll find it odd that I've suddenly rekindled my friendship with Mac, considering I've been a social hermit the whole time we've been back in Stakesville, but she trusts anyone from the old Famous Five more than she would ever trust me, so she won't question it. I'll return home tomorrow afternoon like nothing ever happened.

I wash my empty bowl, dry it and put it away. The kitchen is spotless. I scribble a note and leave it pinned to the fridge: *Decided to walk to Nicky's today. See you at 4 x*

By quarter to seven, my teeth are cleaned, my outfit is perfect and my makeup is done. I slip back into my room to grab my bag and sneak out through the back door.

It's that easy.

I told Cal to meet me at the bottom of the driveway to avoid any chance of being caught. Sure enough, right on seven, his car appears around the corner and pulls over on the shoulder right at our turnoff. I've barely clicked my seatbelt on when we're off again.

'Hi,' I say.

'Hi,' he says.

And then we're both silent.

At this hour, Stakesville is sleepier than ever: there's not a single person on the main street. It's an overcast day, and the flags on the streetlamps flutter slowly in a lazy breeze. It's like the post-apocalypse scene in a sci-fi western. I'm half-expecting a tumbleweed to blow out onto the road in front of us.

I put my feet up on the dashboard.

'Take your feet off the dashboard,' Callum says.

I take my feet off the dashboard.

'Average weather,' I say as we pass the sign that says, *You're leaving Stakesville . . . safe travels!*

And good riddance, I think.

'Mm.'

'I wonder if it'll be like this in Wellington.'

'Maybe.'

'Weather's pretty changeable up there.'

'I guess so.'

'I haven't been to Queenstown airport in *years*,' I say. 'Not since we first moved to New Zealand. When we landed, I fully thought we were going to crash into the mountains. I cried.'

Callum doesn't say anything.

I lose my patience.

'So, are we just going to politely ignore each other this whole trip? Because I'm certainly getting that vibe.'

Finally, Callum meets my eye, and it's not a look I want to see. His whole face is hard, chiselled with annoyance.

'This trip isn't us pretending to be friends,' Callum says — practically spits. We're far out of Stakesville now, hurtling past corn-coloured hills. Behind them are the mountains, silhouetted in the early-morning sky. Everything always looks so much more dramatic at this time of day. 'You're with me because I had no other choice, Zelle, not because I *want* you here.'

Cal's eyes are fixed on the road, but the expression in them is clear. His face is so foreign. I don't like it. I should be able to read everything: his gestures, his expressions, his gaze. Know him and understand him as well as I know myself.

It's like I'm with a stranger.

I suppose I *am* with a stranger.

'There's a difference between *friends* and being an outright dickhead,' I say, folding my arms across my chest.

Cal just rolls his eyes.

Several more minutes pass. Ten? Fifteen? As scenic as the road is, it starts to get boring when you know it's all you're going to see for the next hour and a half. We're hardly a quarter of the way into the drive and already I'm getting restless.

I reach into my bag and grab a packet of Haribos. They're my faithful stand-bys.

'Want one?' I say, stuffing a red gummy into my mouth.

'No.'

I sigh.

This is going to be a long day.

CALLUM

I knew this was a bad idea.

I told Mum and Kate that I was going to spend the weekend with Finn. A road trip to Alexandra to stay at Finn's mum's house. At least it's not entirely a lie. Mum was chill about it, anyway. But now I've got two days — thirty-six hours — stuck with Zelle. So far we haven't even made it through *one*. We drive in starchy silence, Zelle sitting with her feet on the dashboard (after I *told* her not to — there's mud all over the vinyl now) and demolishing a whole packet of Haribo gummy bears. She's staring out the window and her mind seems far away. Me, I'm thinking about the last time I made this drive: my interview for broadcasting school all those weeks ago. If I'd known what was coming, I would've crashed the car into the river.

We arrive at the airport almost two hours before our flight. Okay, so maybe leaving at seven *was* a bit overkill, but 'better safe than sorry' is the motto of my life. I pay for overnight parking, grab my bag from the boot and walk with Zelle into the domestic terminal. We go straight through security and to our gate.

We don't speak.

Now it feels like I've been here for hours. Days. Months. Like my whole life has been inside Gate 14, sitting in silence next to Zelle Bachmann.

I check my phone for notifications. There's nothing from the group chat and nothing from Finn. I refresh my Messenger page over and over, waiting for a message to appear. I know it's up to me to make the first move, but I don't know what to say.

'What's wrong?' Zelle says. She's obviously been watching me.

I side-eye her. 'Nothing.' I hate how even now Zelle can read my emotions. That I'm still that transparent to her.

She folds her arms. 'I always know when you're lying, Cal.'

'How many times do I have to tell you?' I say, suddenly, hopelessly enraged. 'We're not *mates*. We're not *friends*. This isn't meant to be *fun*. Why do you think I would *want* to tell you anything?'

Zelle is now suddenly, hopelessly enraged too. It's easy to know when Zelle's angry: her nostrils flare, her cheeks flush red. I've seen her get mad so often, her furious face is imprinted in my memory. It used to scare me. It doesn't now.

'That's not fair,' she spits. 'We might not be friends,

but that doesn't give you an excuse to treat me like shit. Especially when I've made this entire weekend possible.'

'Oh, come on. Do you need reminding? You told the whole school about my relationship with Eli. And not to mention how you reacted that summer—'

'For God's sake, Callum!' Zelle shouts. An elderly couple with orange tans and Birkenstocks look over. 'I know I messed up, and I know I don't deserve to have you forgive me, but you're not perfect in all of this either. Remember what *you* did that summer? Remember how much of a shitty friend *you* were?'

Oh.

Right.

Well.

That's not the comeback I was expecting.

I drum my fingers against my jeans, staring out at the full panorama of the Remarkables. A plane sits nearby on the tarmac.

'When you first started seeing Eli, it was like I didn't exist to you anymore,' she says. 'You didn't tell me about it for *months*. You kept the whole thing a secret from me.'

'You don't have the right to know *everything*, Zelle. I'm allowed to have secrets.'

'Not when you let our friendship go to ruin because you enjoyed the power of having a secret and you were too selfish to let me in. My parents were breaking up. It was messy. You *knew* that. And you weren't there. Because it wasn't as important as Eli.' She looks over at me, her eyes glassy. 'My life wasn't going so well at the time, you know.

But you never even bothered to ask me how I was.'

'You never told me.'

'A better friend wouldn't have needed me to do that.' She meets my eyes. 'A better friend would've asked.'

There's a roar outside as a plane takes off.

'I'm sorry,' I say.

'I shouldn't have said those things to you that day you told me about Eli,' she says. 'But I'm not the only one in the wrong. Maybe if you'd been a better friend, it never would have happened.'

I think back to that day in late January, the day I felt like my world had well and truly ended.

We were less than a week out from school starting. Nearly two months since the first time I'd kissed Eli in secret, the first of many secret afternoons spent together. And then—

'I don't think we should do this anymore, Cal,' Eli said.

We were at the lake, sunning ourselves after swimming, our towels spread out on the moon-like rock of the shore. Later, the rest of the Famous Five would join us, but we came early. Eli's idea.

'What?'

'School's about to start,' he said, 'and no one needs to know what we did this summer. It was just a bit of fun, right? We were just messing around. But I think we should stop.'

I sat up, feeling like I'd been sucker-punched in the stomach. My eyes filled with unwanted tears. 'It wasn't messing around to me,' I said quietly.

Eli shrugged. 'I'm sorry, Cal,' he said. 'But I never wanted anything more out of this.'

I never wanted anything more. I never wanted you. I never wanted this.

I rode my bike straight from the lake to Zelle's house that day. She opened the front door, we sat down on the porch, and I blurted it all out. I'd never needed her more than I did then. She was the strong one, the brave one. The one who could make everything better.

But she didn't. 'God, Callum, are you listening to yourself right now?' she said. 'You're fourteen. You're not in love. You're just a kid.'

'You don't understand.'

'You're being *so* pathetic right now, you know that?'

I sniffed.

And then I stood up.

'Why are you such a bitch?' I said.

The shock on her face was clear. She stood up too. She was taller than me back then. 'What the hell, Callum?'

'Why are you never supportive? Why do you always act like I'm stupid?' An unfamiliar rage swept through me, wild and uncontrolled and dangerous. 'I've never told you about this, and this is how you react?'

'I already knew!' Zelle shouted. 'I knew, Callum. I've known all along. Remember Christmas Eve, Cal? I was in tears when I called you up. Dad had finally announced he was leaving us. You didn't answer, so I went over to yours. Turns out you were too busy making out with Eli to pick up my calls.'

A chill went through me.

'So, quite frankly, I don't care about what happened with Eli, because it doesn't matter,' she spat, and somehow the words were even worse than Eli telling me he didn't want me anymore. '*I* matter. *Our* friendship matters.'

'No, it doesn't,' I said.

Zelle froze.

'What?' she said, so quietly, a tiny voice full of fear.

'You're jealous and possessive and controlling,' I said, 'and you don't care about me. You just want someone to boss around. There's no *us* in our friendship, it's all about you. Everything. *You* get to be the one in charge. *You* get to have all the problems. *You* get to decide what's important. You're selfish, Zelle. And I'm sick of it.'

'That's not true,' she said. 'You know I care about you, Callum.'

'I don't care,' I said. 'I don't want to hear it anymore, Zelle.'

And I turned around.

And I walked away.

'So, what?' Zelle called after me. 'We're not friends anymore?'

I didn't answer.

'Don't be stupid, Cal,' she said. 'You know the only reason you have any friends at all is because of me. Why do you think Eli rejected you? Because you're nothing, Callum. Nothing and no one. He probably only pretended to like you because he pitied you.'

I didn't react. I got on my bike and cycled home. I texted

the Famous Five that I wasn't going to the swimming hole. Zelle said, *me neither*. Fox and Mac said we'd go another time.

Eli didn't respond. He was already dead.

And that was the last time I saw Zelle.

There's a weird heat behind my eyes and I have to blink several times to make it go away. When I finally look at Zelle, her eyes are misty, too.

'I wish I'd been better,' I say.

Zelle crosses one leg over the other, examining the soles of her boots. 'Me too,' she says.

'So,' I say. 'We're settled on the fact that we've both been absolute arseholes to each other. Truce?'

Zelle sits up. 'Really?'

I shrug. 'I mean, if we're going to be stuck with each other for the next two days, we might as well make the most of it.' I look away. 'I've missed you a lot,' I mutter.

'I've missed you, too,' she says. 'And you know what? A truce sounds good.' She sticks out her pinkie. I stick out mine.

We shake on it.

ZELLE

It's like a weight I didn't even know I was carrying has been whipped right off my shoulders. I feel as light as if I'm made of air. It's so much more bearable standing in line for boarding knowing that Cal doesn't hate my existence.

Or at least holding off from hating my existence until we get back to Stakesville.

Either way, I'll take it.

It's just past eleven when our flight leaves. Mum hasn't messaged me yet; she would have seen the note on the fridge telling her I'd decided to walk to work, and she hasn't come calling to see whether I've fled the country. That's new. Mum is far from relaxed when it comes to me, but the past couple of weeks she's definitely loosened up. A flicker of guilt pangs in me. She'd absolutely freak if she knew what I was doing right now. I'd get in the worst trouble of my life.

It would be worth it, though. For Cal.

Callum naps beside me. As we swoop over the Cook Strait and the pilot announces we're preparing for landing, I get a fizzy feeling in my stomach. An exhilarating kind of nervousness, like when you're at the peak of a rollercoaster, or you've successfully snuck out of the house without waking your parents. I'm coming home.

I haven't told my friends I'll be here, and I'm not going to. They'll definitely be partying tonight, and I can use their location on Snapchat to find out where. My plan is to surprise them. Luka, especially. We'll hug, we'll drink — because it's been two months since I've touched a drop of alcohol, and I know my limits, and I'm *fine* — and it'll be like I never left. It'll be normal.

God, how I miss feeling *normal*.

The landing is classic Wellington. Cal's eyes snap open as we shudder on the tarmac; his face is slightly green.

'We made it,' I say.

He peers past my shoulder to the view outside. It's just the airport and the hills behind, but his lips curve up into a smile. 'We made it,' he repeats. 'We're in Wellington. We flew to fucking *Wellington*. And no one even knows.' His jaw drops an inch. 'Shit, Zelle.'

And for the first time in three years, we laugh together.

The bus from the airport lets us off at Lambton Quay, which is bustling with Saturday shoppers. God, I've missed it. We take the steps that connect to The Terrace. Mum's apartment building is straight across the street.

'Where's your place?' Cal says, drinking in the buildings.

I point.

'*Really*?'

I shrug, feeling embarrassed. 'It's a pretty nice place,' I say.

'*Pretty nice*,' he repeats. 'Let me guess, you're in the penthouse too.'

I don't answer.

'Oh, come on,' he says. 'I forgot your parents are world famous and stinking rich.'

I bristle. I hate talking about money. It's easy to forget, but there's no one in Stakesville you could consider rich. Not in this sense. 'My parents are split up,' I say, 'and my mum hasn't done an exhibition in, like, five years. We're not driving superyachts and Jaguars.'

At least Mum isn't. I don't know about Dad. Much as I hate it, he's always earned more than Mum, always been the more famous one. I'm sure he loves spoiling his girlfriend. Giving her a reason to stay, since looks and personality are lacking.

I use my swipe card to unlock the main apartment doors. We step into the elevator and go up to Floor 10. We turn a corner and there's us: suite 10B. I put my key in the lock.

'Wow,' Cal says. 'So this is where you've been hiding out the last three years.' He steps into the living area, where floor-to-ceiling windows showcase the Kelburn hills. It smells a little musty in here, so I open up the balcony door. Cal takes his wonder outside.

'God, Mistakesville's a downgrade compared to here,'

he says. 'Why'd you give up *this*?'

I pretend not to hear him.

While Callum stands and takes in the view, I send Mum my pre-prepared text. *don't worry about picking me up today, I'm going to spend the night at mac's. she can drop me home tomorrow.*

She replies almost immediately with a thumbs-up. Too easy.

I head up the stairs to my old room. There's three bedrooms up here: mine, Mum's, and the spare, which Mum used as her studio. My room is exactly the same as I left it: the fairy lights strung across the ceiling, my desk cluttered with books and old makeup, the Polaroids pinned to the wall. I'd forgotten the photo of Eli was there. Blutacked above my desk, small and inconspicuous, it's a printout of an old image I'd found on my phone.

'Who's that?' Tabitha asked me once.

'Oh, just an old friend from Stakesville,' I said.

'An old friend?' she said. 'The only one to make it to your photo wall?'

'I told you, I was a loser back then,' I said, trying to joke, but my heart hurt and my smile was false. After that I always took down the photo whenever I knew I had friends coming over.

I don't hear Callum until he's right behind me.

'Christ, Cal!' I say. 'Some warning would be nice.'

But it's too late. 'You have his photo,' he says, his voice pitched with an emotion I can't decipher. Disbelief, maybe.

'I didn't forget about you, you know,' I say. 'I still

thought of everyone. And I thought a lot about Eli.'

'Yeah,' Cal says. 'Me too.'

We're quiet.

'Anyway,' I say at last. 'I don't know about you, but I am fucking *ravenous*. Should we go find lunch?'

'Lunch sounds good,' Cal says, and it feels like we've broken another barrier, somehow.

Turns out I'm the only one who's ravenous. I demolish my meal while Cal barely touches his overpriced but iconic Wellington BLT.

'Aren't you going to eat that?' I say, pointing at his sandwich with my fork. I snag a chip from his plate while I'm at it.

He pushes his plate away. 'I feel sick.'

'About the panel?'

'Amongst other things.'

I snag another chip, chewing off the end and holding it in my mouth like it's a cigarette. 'Finn?' I say, waggling my eyebrows. It feels safe enough now to bring him up. 'How's that going?'

'Not great,' Cal says, nibbling on a chip. 'He's mad at me. So is everyone else, actually.'

'Fox and Mac?'

He nods.

'Why?'

He looks out to the din of Cuba Street, the thrift stores and record stores and restaurants with prices that make your eyes water, families and couples and clusters of punky teens crowding the footpath. 'They're mad that I never told them about Eli,' he says, and I flinch, knowing that's on me. 'And that I haven't told them what's going on with Finn. Which is a whole other mess in itself.' He looks back at me. 'And they don't know I'm here, of course. Or what happened at the broadcasting school interview.'

'What happened at the interview?' I ask, feeling a lot like Mr Appleby right now, but too emboldened by bacon and caffeine to pull back.

Callum takes a sip of his flat white and shakes his head, his glasses sliding down his nose. 'It was horrible,' he says.

'I'm sure it wasn't that bad.' This is Cal, after all, whose standards for himself are about as high as the Royal Family's. Anything short of perfect in his book is labelled a disaster.

'You don't understand. It was awful.'

'So, what? You were nervous and gave an average interview. You didn't sell yourself enough. Now you've got a second chance, you know exactly what to do. You're a charmer, Cal. It won't be hard for you to convince them why they should let you through.'

'I didn't even *do* the interview, Zelle,' he says in a garbled rush. 'I ran out.'

It takes a moment for my brain to process this. 'You . . . what?'

'I ran out,' he repeats. 'I got called in, threw up, and then I just . . . ran.'

'What? Why?'

He stares at me a long moment. He pushes up his

glasses. 'You'd just texted me saying you were coming back.'

'You walked out of the interview because of me?' Noxious guilt washes over me so strongly I want to be sick. I suddenly regret eating lunch as enthusiastically as I did.

'Yes. No. I don't know. I was freaking out.'

'You shouldn't have done that,' I say. I feel weirdly, unwantedly angry.

'You'd been gone for three years, and then out of the blue you told me you were moving back. How could I *not* freak out?' He seems to sense how riled I'm getting, because he lets his face relax. 'Look, it's not your fault. It's not like you knew it was a bad time. And it's my fault for letting it get in the way of my interview.'

His words barely reach me, though, because I'm thinking, *It's your fault, it's all your fault, it's always your fucking fault*. It's my fault that I ruined my friendship with Cal and broke his trust and caused Eli—

My phone starts ringing.

'Oh, shit,' I say, looking down.

'What? Who is it?' Cal says.

It's Mum.

CALLUM

'Hi, Mum.' Zelle's voice is a forced calm, and the hard set of her jaw and the way her eyes refuse to meet mine tells me everything I need to know. We've been caught. 'I'm at work.'

'No, you're not,' roars the tinny voice on the other end, and Zelle presses the phone more firmly to her ear. But Anneke could be heard from across the Tasman. *'Tell me where you are. Really.'*

'Mama, what the *hell*?' It's the angriest I've ever heard Zelle. I can't imagine in a million years ever speaking to my mother like that. I don't think I would survive. Zelle turns away from me.

'I'd just driven down to Nicky's to drop you off some lunch,' I hear Anneke say, *'right when I'd got your text about not coming to pick you up today. And then I go into Nicky's and she tells me you're not here, that you called in sick with a stomach*

bug. So you've lied about where you are. And I bet you're not at Mac's house either.'

'We went to Queenstown for the day,' Zelle spills in a rush. 'There's the fireworks show on tonight, and we just wanted to go for the day, and I knew you wouldn't let me miss work, or even let me go in the first place, even though I'm nearly an adult, for God's sake—'

'I'm coming to get you,' Anneke says. *'Right now.'*

Zelle gazes at me with wild, panicked eyes, and even I'm stumped. Zelle is the queen of getting into trouble, sneaking around, pulling out lies like rabbits from a hat and getting away scot free. Why is she faltering? Why is she the most panicked I've ever seen her? And why is Anneke freaking out so much, anyway? Zelle's parents were always the opposite of strict. Hell, Zelle spent the first nine years of her life globetrotting in the adult world; she was practically born independent. It's not like Anneke to keep such tight tabs on her.

Something's not right.

'No,' she says. 'No, don't do that.'

'Too bad.'

'You can't!' Zelle bursts. 'You can't, because I'm in Wellington, okay? I'm in Wellington, and I'm staying at the apartment, and you can't keep me from living my own life, and I'll be back tomorrow afternoon, and I'm *fine*—'

'No!' The panic in her voice, even louder than her anger, sends a tingle of dread down my spine. *'You better not be seeing your friends. And you definitely better not be drinking—'*

Zelle cuts her off. She's breathing heavy, her fingers trembling.

And I know that something is very, very wrong.

'Zelle,' I say slowly. 'What's going on?'

She doesn't meet my eye. 'Nothing.'

'Why was your mum so freaked out?'

'It's not your business, Cal.'

'Why did she mention your friends? And drinking?'

'For God's sake, it's nothing, Callum! Will you drop it?'

But it's not nothing, not from the way Zelle marches us back to the apartment and won't meet my eye. I've got just over two hours until the panel discussion, and I'm shitting bricks. Maybe it's my already-jangled nerves making me catastrophise, but I *know* Zelle's hiding something. Something important. Which isn't out of character for her.

I want to trust her. God, I wish I could. Even with everything she's done, even after Joe Rooney's party, I've kept a flicker of hope in her, believed that she could change. I've always thought Mac and Fox were wrong about Zelle. Too harsh on her, too unwilling to understand. Her leaving was the second-worst thing to ever happen to me, after Eli dying. But losing all hope in my former best friend somehow feels worse than losing her physical presence.

'I know you're hiding something,' I say, as Zelle swipes the keycard to her building and we head towards the elevator. 'You're always hiding something.'

'I'm not, Callum!'

'Why can't you just tell me the truth?' I say, washed over with desperation. 'For once in your life, why can't you tell the fucking truth?'

'Because there's nothing to tell!' Zelle shouts, just as the elevator doors slide open to our floor. She leaps out and fumbles to unlock the apartment. 'A couple of months ago, I was in the hospital because I drank too much, and Mum thinks that since then I need to be hand-held like a fucking toddler, because I made *one* mistake, *once,* and everyone acts like I have a problem but no one's ever asked me and I don't have a fucking problem and I'm *sick* of everyone acting like they're in charge of my own goddamned life!'

She looks so small inside her too-big living room, the hills of the city behind her like some cinematic backdrop. Her voice cracks and tears are welling in her eyes. At first I'm too stunned to speak. Not just because I'm still processing Zelle's outburst, but because I feel things falling into place.

'You said you moved back to Stakesville to renovate The Sanctuary,' I say. 'And to finally make peace.'

'We *did,*' she says. But I see the fight go out of her.

'You're a liar,' I say.

I know this isn't the right response. There's a part of me that's ringing alarm bells at the fact that Zelle is crying so much, that knows there's something wrong here, a problem that's bigger than the both of us. There's a part of me that wants to take Zelle in my arms and let her explain whatever it is that's going on.

There's a bigger part of me, though, that's angry. Because maybe Fox and Mac are right.

'We had to come back someday,' she sniffs.

'But the reason you finally did was because you have a drinking problem,' I say. 'Would you *ever* have come back, Zelle? Or would you have kept pretending that part of your life never happened because you're lucky enough to have that option? Were you ever planning to talk to me again?'

'I do *not* have a drinking problem!' she yells. 'Don't ever say that again, Callum!'

But she doesn't say anything else.

I shake my head slowly. 'Every time we try to make this work, you screw me over,' I say, rage boiling red in the bottom of my stomach. 'I'm sick of it, Zelle. Everything you are is a lie. No wonder you had to come back – you messed up your life here too. That's who you are. You destroy everything. And then you run away because you don't care. You haven't changed, Zelle. And you never will.'

'Why are you being so horrible about this?' Her voice is too loud, and I'm certain the neighbours will be able to hear us, but I don't bother to tell her to be quiet and I don't answer her question. I know I have the opportunity here to back down, to put my head back over my heart, piece things together before they're irreparably splintered apart. But I don't. I can't.

And maybe that makes me just as bad.

'You know, I always wondered why you'd chosen me as your friend,' I say. 'I thought I didn't deserve you. That you were too good. But *you* don't deserve *me*.'

She stares at me. Glassy-eyed with tear-stained cheeks.

Strands of blue hair stuck to her forehead in sticky clumps. She looks like a mess. She looks like the poster face of guilt.

'Get out,' she says.

So I do.

ZELLE

Not long after Callum leaves, I do too.

I have a shower first, though, soothing my puffy eyes and swollen lips. A bottle of merlot sits on the bathroom sink. Mum has always kept the key to her liquor cabinet in her underwear drawer — she obviously never thought I'd be back to retrieve it. I hate reds, but that's all she has.

My weeks of sobriety have done wonders for my tolerance. Only halfway through the bottle the fizzy feeling hits me like a freight train. I do my makeup in the mirror, focusing hard to keep steady with my increasingly clumsy hand, turning myself beautiful, the best I've ever looked. I don't have any product for my hair, but I tousle the waves with my fingers and admire the way the curls fall down my shoulders. I'm the life of the party, the girl with the loudest voice and the best stories and the funniest anecdotes, and I'm crazy and I'm wild and I'm

Zelle Bachmann, only seventeen, daughter of one of this century's most iconic artists, and everyone loves me. And maybe I have a problem, but it's better than facing what I feel.

On Snap Maps I can see Luka, Tabitha, Lucy and Anahera are all together, drinking at Luka's flat. I grab a second bottle from Mum's cabinet and slide it into my jacket pocket. It's nearly five, not even an hour since I told Callum to get out.

At the door I hesitate for a moment, vaguely aware of the absurdity of my plan. At some point Cal will know that I've gone. I can't get away from him, not really, so what's the point in trying?

No, I might not be able to disappear. But at least I can forget.

I lock the door behind me and stride out into the evening light.

CALLUM

Halfway towards broadcasting school, I'm struck by how badly I've fucked things up. Now that the anger has subsided, regret seeps in and reality hits: she must have a pretty bad problem if that's the reason she came back to Mistakesville. Still, I'm struggling to make the numbers add up. Can teenagers even *have* drinking problems? Most of us have only just started drinking, if at all. How can you develop an alcohol problem before you're even the legal age to drink?

I could've let Zelle speak. But instead I made it about myself.

If I were a better friend, I would've listened.

If I were a better friend, I would've set my anger aside.

If I were a better friend, I'd be there with her right now, not walking towards broadcasting school like the selfish prick I am, leaving Zelle upset and vulnerable.

And alone in a city full of alcohol, on a Saturday night, with the friends Anneke so strongly warned her against seeing.

Oh, God.

I call Zelle. The phone rings and rings, before it cuts off to the monotone robot voice, telling me to leave a message.

I try to be grateful that at least I didn't go straight to voicemail.

'Hey,' I say. 'Look, I'm sorry. I was a complete dickhead before. Just . . . let me know you're okay, yeah?'

I wait a few minutes, knowing how unlikely it is that she'll call me back but hoping somehow she will.

I keep walking, trying hard not to panic. Of course she'd want space from me. It hasn't even been an hour. Of course she's not picking up the phone. It's probably best for us to spend some time apart, cooling down, then I'll go back and we can talk properly. She'll need to let me back in, anyway. Not to mention we've got a flight to catch together tomorrow afternoon.

It'll be fine.

I hope.

I'm really sorry, I text, basically repeating what I said over voicemail.

I didn't mean what I said

please let me know you're OK

I put my phone away and try my best not to think about it.

My heart lurches when I see the broadcasting school up

ahead. The modern glass building, the sign in bold letters. It's just after five. I cross the street, push my way through the groups of noisy teenagers and parents clutching open-day brochures, and search the lobby until I find a woman with a lanyard who looks like she's waiting for someone.

We make eye contact, she waves, and for a moment I almost forget about everything that's happened in the past hour: I'm here, at broadcasting school, and while I'm a bundle of nerves they're good nerves, excited nerves, because here is my opportunity to redeem myself, to show the school that I'm worth it—

'Callum?' Jazz shakes my hand, firm and brisk, and pulls a second lanyard from her pocket. 'Lovely to finally meet you in person,' she says. 'Wear this. It'll show you're allowed to be backstage.'

There's nothing to boost an ego quite like a lanyard.

'How was the flight here? Where are you staying?' Jazz asks, leading me towards a makeshift stage, haphazard rows of empty chairs in front of it.

'Good,' I say, my fleeting bubbliness replaced by a sinking sense of doom. 'I'm, uh, staying at a family friend's place.'

'Here's our *green room,*' Jazz says, opening a door behind the stage that's marked *Authorised access only*. 'We've got water and snacks, so feel free to help yourself. And here are the other panel members. This is Laurence, the vice-president of Politics in Media, Ibrahim, the MC, and Kit, who's an alumnus of the school and is now a political reporter for the *Guardian*—'

Three figures on a sinking orange couch wave and smile, while Jazz continues talking. 'So, anyway, tonight's basically meant to promote our club, show them the kinds of issues we discuss and what we're all about. We've got, like, just under forty minutes until the panel starts? So make yourself at home, have a chat, have something to eat—'

I turn to the trestle table behind me and pour a plastic cup to the brim with chilled water. The all-too familiar nausea gnawing at my insides warns against the idea of snacks. I'm feeling too wound up to strike up a conversation with the others, so I pull out my phone. Zelle still hasn't replied. Do I text again? Try another call? Then I remember I've still got her on Snapchat. The little cartoon version of herself shows up on the satellite map of Wellington, so I zoom in, and—

She's not at the apartment. Far from it, actually. Somewhere deep in the hills of Kelburn, going God knows where.

I call her. The phone rings three times before cutting out. I call again, and the same thing happens. When I try a third time, I go straight to voicemail.

'I have to go,' I tell Jazz.

She looks at me like I've just dropped dog shit at her feet and called it a Christmas present. 'What?'

'Something's happened, and I need to go,' I say.

'But the panel's starting in half an hour.'

'I know. I'm sorry. But I can't.'

'This is your only opportunity.'

'And this is more important,' I snap. I sweep my gaze across the room, where Laurence, Ibrahim and Kit are watching me open-mouthed. I take off my lanyard and leave it on the table. 'Sorry,' I say.

And then I run from the room and out of the building.

I have to find Zelle.

ZELLE

I'm nearly at Luka's when my phone rings.

I know without looking that it's Callum and I let the call ring out. A minute later, it buzzes again, and I pull my phone out of my jacket pocket. My balance is off-kilter and everything tilts, and my fingers are clumsy as I unlock the screen.

I'm really sorry

I didn't mean what I said

please let me know you're OK

He doesn't deserve an answer.

My head is spinning and my thoughts are swirling, but I know the way to Luka's by heart. His flat's in the depths of Aro Valley, down the hill over the other side of uni. It's an old part of town, shoddy student flats in historic houses left to rot in the gloom. Luka calls the suburb *quaint*. I call it a shithole.

Cal calls again. And again. The third time he tries, I'm so irritated I decline the call as soon as his name pops up. How hard is it for him to get the memo?

The sky is pink streaked with sunset, and the noise of a party drifts down to the street. Luka's flat is on the bottom floor of a massive three-storey colonial house. The paint on the weatherboards is peeling and the outside deck feels one misstep away from collapse. It's a dump, but at least that means the landlord doesn't care what happens to it so we have free range. I stumble up the terraced pathway and bang on the door.

Some shitty DnB is blasting, and it takes several knocks before anyone notices. I feel a stab of nervousness then, and muster up my best smile.

Anahera opens the door. She's wearing a wraparound crop top that offers barely more coverage than a bra, and a miniskirt with knee-high boots. Her dark skin sparkles with body glitter, and her hair bounces like a cloud. She looks surprised, but not exactly in a good way.

'Zelle?'

'Hey!' I say. Since she's not moving, I step past her into the doorway. 'Long time, no see! How have you been? How's uni?'

'What are you doing here? Aren't you living down south?'

'I'm back here for the weekend,' I say, and take a swig from my wine. 'Just thought I'd come remind you of my existence.' I laugh, but my clumsy words sound like an accusation, and Anahera's eyebrows knit together. She's sipping from a can of Vodka Cruiser, so at least she's probably as drunk as I am.

'This is Luka's flat,' she says. 'He didn't know you were coming.'

'Well, surprise,' I say, not understanding why she seems so cautious, but also not really caring. I'm back in my element, my home. I push past her into the living room, where the couches have been pushed up against the wall and there are bottles littered on the ground and a chunky speaker is blasting music from the corner, and there's Luka, sitting on one of the couches, with a random girl on top of him, making out like there's no one watching, his eager hands dancing over her sparkly-orange dress.

'Luka,' I say. My voice cuts through the music.

The girl turns around. It's Tabitha, her hair freshly turned blonde. She gapes at me and clambers off Luka like I'm the chastity police. Luka looks similarly aghast.

I can't speak.

'Zelle?' he says. But then his face shifts, showing something like anger. 'What are you doing?'

'What are *you* doing?' I shoot back.

'How the hell did you get here? Don't you live in, like, Dunedin?'

'So, since when did you two start hooking up?' I say, wagging my finger between them. 'Tonight? Five minutes ago?'

'Tabby's my girlfriend, Zelle,' Luka says.

'Since when?'

'Since a month ago.'

'And you never thought to tell me.'

'I think you should leave,' Luka says.

'Why?' I stand up straighter. 'I came here to surprise you! Ta-da! Remember me? Your friend? The one you've forgotten to talk to for the past month?'

All my old friends, plus others I've met from previous parties or through friends of friends, stand and watch and say nothing. Anahera is glaring.

Luka stands up from the couch. I'd forgotten just how much taller than me he is, and he looks as imposing as when I first met him. I take a step backwards, almost falling over an empty beer bottle.

'You're really drunk,' Luka says, making it sound like a bad thing.

'And you're being a cunt,' I say. 'What's the deal with you all? Why are you acting like I'm, I don't know, fucking rabid?'

Luka snatches my hand as if I'm a naughty toddler and drags me outside.

'You need to go,' he says.

I dig the tip of my boot into the dirt. 'Aren't you happy to see me?' I say, aware of how pathetic and whimpering I sound.

'No, Zelle,' he says. 'No, I'm not happy to see you, honestly. Which is why you need to leave.'

'What the *fuck* is wrong with you?' I say. 'What is your problem? Why are you all acting like you're too good for me? Why'd you start ghosting?'

'Because you're a mess, Zelle,' Luka shouts. 'You're not

fun to hang around with. You're a liability and you're an underage alcoholic.'

'I'm *not*.'

'You are.'

'You drink as much as I do!'

'No, I don't,' Luka says. 'Whenever we drink, we get drunk, but you always take it too far. Every time. One of us is always having to walk you home or listen to you cry about whatever problem you're drinking to forget or having to call you an ambulance when you pass out in a gutter. It's immature.'

'But you're my friends.'

'Sure, at first Anahera said you were cool,' Luka says. 'Even though you were still in school. But that was before we realised how much of a wreck you are. It's embarrassing.'

'So.' I breathe in long, deep through my nose. 'You don't want me here? You don't even want to be my friend?'

He shakes his head. 'Please, Zelle, it would be easier if you just left.'

An all-too-familiar feeling rises up in me: a blood-curdling anger, untamed and destructive. I know what lies beneath it, but I don't want to let myself feel it. Anger is active. But hurt? It's passive. It's paralysing. And once I fall down into it, I'm not sure I can lift myself up again.

I push past Luka and march back into his lounge room.

'I have an announcement,' I say, and everyone stops, and to my satisfaction some of them even look a little bit scared. 'And that is, fuck you. Fuck all of you. You're a bunch of useless, selfish, stupid narcissists. I hope you rot in the fucking depths of hell.'

I spin a slow circle around the room. Lucy, Tabitha, Luka – none of them meets my eye. No one does. Except for Anahera. She rolls her eyes and her lip curls up into a smirk.

And that's it.

I take a step forward until I'm close enough to kiss her, and pour the rest of my red wine down her skimpy white top.

She screams.

'What the actual *fuck*?!' she shouts, and you'd think she'd been stabbed. The wine blooms like a bloodstain down her top and over her exposed midriff, dripping onto her skirt. Around me there's screaming and yelling and shouting. I make a dash for Anahera's box of Cruisers.

'Thanks for the drinks!' I say on my way out. Which is when the tears start and don't stop.

CALLUM

Finding Zelle is nothing short of a mission.

Her location on Snap Maps hasn't changed, but my navigation skills are iffy at the best of times, and I don't know the first thing about Wellington. Turns out Uber won't let you sign up if you're under eighteen, and I don't want to risk getting on a bus.

It takes me over half an hour to find where Zelle supposedly is. Immediately I can tell I'm in studentville: if the run-down houses and overflowing recycling bins weren't enough of a clue, the music blaring from every second house certainly is. I feel far too out of place and far too sober to be here.

I turn up the street that I hope is the right one. A pack of students holding RTD boxes and dancing down the footpath are singing a rendition of 'Wonderwall' that could put an entire football stadium to shame.

'Join us!' one of them says.

I bustle past and continue my way up the hill.

'Loser!'

Their voices fade into the night like smoke.

I zoom in on Zelle's emoji, which is perched on a house just off the street and up a precarious-looking hill. I look across the road and am flooded with relief when I think I spot it: a big white-weatherboard house at the top of a snaking path that looks like it's designed to trip up clumsy feet. The dark has fully sunk in now, and I shine my phone torch down at the ground to light the way. I can hear music drifting from the bottom floor of the house, voices. Panic constricts my chest. What if I've got the wrong place? What if I knock and whoever's inside refuses to speak to me, this random clueless kid appearing on their doorstep? What if they're murderers? What if they think *I'm* a murderer? What if Zelle is out there somewhere in this dark and twisting valley, alone or hurt or *being* hurt or in danger or dead—

I bang on the door, loud. Figures move behind the frosted glass. Backlit by green strobe lighting, a silhouette approaches. The door opens, and a tall, imposing-looking guy gazes down at me, the epitome of straight, alpha-male hyper-masculinity. I almost turn around and bolt back down the path.

'Do I know you?' he says, partially bored, partially aggressive. Is he murderer material? I'm too intimidated to make a judgement.

'Is Zelle here?' I blurt. (*Why* do I sound like that?)

The guy frowns, but I can tell he knows who I'm talking about.

'Who the hell are you?' he says.

'Do you know Zelle? Has she been here?'

The guy looks at me hard, his expression on the verge of an eyeroll. 'She left,' he says. 'About half an hour ago.'

'Where?'

'I don't know.' He sips from a can of beer. 'She was drunk.'

'And you let her go off alone?'

(Oh God, my prissiness is going to get me decked.)

'Who even *are* you, mate?' he says.

'A friend,' I say, 'and, you know, this is pretty important, so if you could actually help me out, that would be appreciated.'

The guy rolls his shoulders back like a peacock, seeming to remind me of our height difference, and lets out an irritated sigh. 'Have you tried to call her?' he says.

'She won't answer.' I look up at the sky. 'It's complicated,' I add.

'Luka?' a voice calls out, and a blonde-haired girl in a shimmering orange dress and high heels wobbles towards us. She slinks her arm around the guy's — Luka's — waist. Her glare could melt Arctic ice. 'Who are you?' she says.

'Some guy looking for Zelle,' Luka says.

The girl does a double-take. 'Are you Eli?' she says. 'The boy from her wall?'

'No,' I say. It feels like another brick has been added to the weight on my chest.

'I could call her from my phone,' Luka says, in a tone that suggests, *I could but I don't want to, and I'm going to try my hardest to make sure I don't have to.*

'She's a fucking psycho,' the girl says. 'She poured red wine all down Anahera's top! And stole her drinks! She's unhinged.'

'And I need to find her,' I snap, and the girl goes quiet.

'See if this works,' Luka says, passing me his phone. He's already called Zelle's number. I hold the phone to my ear and wish for a miracle.

On the fourth ring, she picks up.

'Luka?'

'It's Cal. Where are you?'

I can hear the sound of sipping, Zelle's heavy, laboured breathing clogged with tears. 'Cal? What the hell?' she says.

'Are you okay?'

'What's it to you, Mother?'

I take a deep breath and look up. 'Just tell me where you are,' I say. 'I'll take you home.'

'No,' she says, a fresh sob cracking her throat. 'Don't wanna.'

'Why not?'

'Because everything's broken. And it's all my fault.'

'No, it's not,' I say, and Luka and the girl send me bored looks. 'You're my best friend,' I add, and it feels like the truest thing I know. And Zelle only cries harder.

'I'm in the bedroom,' she says.

'What?'

'Luka's bedroom.'

'You're . . . here?' I say, and Luka and the girl gasp in panic, as if they've just been told there's an armed intruder in their house. I push past them into the living room, past wide-eyed onlookers and a girl with a red-wine stain all down her top who looks like she's been the victim of a bloodbath. I can't help but feel a smirk of satisfaction. Down the hallway that's just to the left of the living room are three closed doors. I open the first one I come to.

Huddled in the corner, with her legs pressed tight to her chest, is Zelle.

'Leave the light off,' she says. Her words slosh and crash into each other. 'How'd you find me?'

'Snap Maps. Luka said you'd left.'

'I did,' she says. 'To go in through the back.'

I stifle a laugh. Then the door behind me crashes open, the harsh light assaults my eyes, and Luka and the girl enter in a fury that's absolutely uncalled for. 'What the fuck?' Luka barks. 'Get out, Zelle.'

'We were just leaving,' I say.

'Where's my phone?'

I throw his phone onto the unmade bed. 'C'mon, Zelle,' I say, reaching out my arm.

Like a reluctant toddler, she clutches my wrist, her grip weak and shaky. In her other hand she's still clasping a can. I try to prise it off her.

'Fuck off!' she says, swiping my hand away. She stumbles to her feet. Bright-red liquid sloshes from the can and onto the carpet as her body crashes into mine. I hold my arm around her waist and half-guide, half-drag her out of the room. Luka and the girl watch on, saying nothing.

'Thanks for your help,' I say.

Zelle bursts into tears on my shoulder.

'S'okay,' I say as we stumble down the path to the street. 'It's okay, Zelle.'

'No, it's not.'

'How do we get home from here?' I say. 'Do you have Uber? Can we call a taxi?'

She's not answering.

'Can I use your phone?' I say, sliding it out of her jacket pocket. 'What's the password?'

But when I look up, she's stumbling away from me, still drinking, and she trips on the kerb and over onto the road, and I see the lights of the car and hear the blare of the horn and I'm yelling, 'Zelle!' at the same time as the brakes squeal and a sickening thud cracks the air and my heart jumps straight out of my chest and I let out a sound halfway between a scream and a sob, and then everything goes very, very quiet.

ZELLE

Cold pavement.

Hot cheek.

Need air.

Need water.

I open my eyes and the light is too much. Animal noises escape my throat. Body hurts. Head hurts. Try to move. Too heavy. A hand on my back. Voices whispering into my ear.

Try to speak. No words. No air.

Standing on the edge of an infinitude. I let it swallow me whole.

ZELLE

When I wake up, the world rushes in.

The fire in my body has dulled to a low flicker, the final embers left in a bonfire. But, God, I feel hollow. And I *hurt*. My ribs, my left arm, the side of my head. I lift a hand to my temple and feel an impressive egg forming above my ear. My head spins and my vision's glittery. An IV-line snakes out of my arm, and I realise with a jolt of déjà vu that I'm in hospital, again.

And that Callum, sitting in a chair at the side of my bed, is watching me.

'Hey,' he says.

'Hey,' I say.

He smiles, his eyes bloodshot, the skin beneath bruised by shadows. He passes me a cup of water, and I down it like it's liquid gold.

'My head hurts,' I say.

He takes my empty cup and places it on the table. 'That'll be the bruising,' he says. 'Don't worry, it's not a concussion. And nothing's broken, either. Just a few bumps and grazes.' He strokes my palm. 'I was so worried, Zelle.'

I bring my hands up to my eyes to cover the tears that leak shamelessly down my cheeks. Tears spill through the gaps in my fingers, soaking my hands, smearing my cheeks a wet, hot mess. God, I remember. I remember it all. Fighting with Callum, telling him to get out. Drinking Mum's merlot. Going to Luka's, only to hear a truth I'd long suspected, only to be left sad and alone and rejected by the only people I had left. Callum, again. The screaming. The car.

And now, here.

I'm so stupid.

'I'm sorry,' I say, too ashamed to look Cal in the eye. 'I'm so, so sorry.'

He reaches over, and, ever so gently, takes my hands and moves them away from my face. 'It's okay,' he says. He strokes my cheeks with his thumbs.

'I have a problem,' I say.

Callum squeezes my hand.

'We'll get through it,' he says.

We.

I never deserved Callum as a friend. He was always too good for me. And after everything I've done, I deserve him even less.

But, right now, despite everything, here he is.

I owe him so much.

Starting with a proper explanation.

'I'm a terrible friend to you,' I say.

Cal shakes his head. 'I shouldn't have got mad at you,' he says. 'I'm sorry.'

I remember now — Cal finding out about my problem, me freaking out. Honestly, what did I expect? It's not like I could've kept it a secret for much longer. Running from the truth never works. I've always known that.

Fresh tears spring to my eyes, and I don't bother to wipe them away this time.

'It's my fault Eli died,' I say. 'That's why I stopped talking to you. Because I figured you must've known that too.'

I'm properly crying now, the type of snot-nosed, great-gulping-sobs type of crying that is completely mortifying. I use my fingers to try to wipe my cheeks, but the tears are flowing far too fast.

Callum, though, is leaning slightly forward in his chair, looking at me hard. 'What?' he says. 'Eli's death was an accident, Zelle.'

'But that day,' I choke, 'that day when Eli broke up with you — I didn't mean those things, Cal. I swear. I only said them because I wanted to hurt you. And if I hadn't said that, if I hadn't ruined everything, we would've gone to the lake with Eli and Fox and Mac like we'd planned, instead of leaving Eli on his own, and he wouldn't have drowned—'

I stop, but not because it's too painful to go on. But because Cal is *laughing*.

'What the hell?' I say. This is by far my deepest, heaviest

secret, and Cal is *laughing* about it?

'Zelle,' he says. 'I've *never* blamed you for Eli's death. Never.'

I don't think I'm hearing quite right.

I sit up a little taller.

'That day, me and Eli were already at the lake,' Cal says. 'We went early, before everyone else, and I asked him if we could finally tell you all about me and him. I didn't want to keep it a secret anymore. But then . . . he told me he didn't want to be with me. So I left, and that's when I went to yours. He was already at the lake by himself. It's not your fault he was alone.'

And maybe it's the hangover, or my aching head, or the fact that I'm still sobbing like a toddler, but it takes a full five seconds before Callum's sentence starts to form meaning in my head.

He's never blamed me.

He's *never blamed me*.

He's . . . never blamed me?

'You've what?' I say, suspended in surreal disbelief.

Cal shakes his head. 'What happened that day was an *accident*,' he says, putting so much more emphasis on the word than I ever thought possible. 'If it was anyone's fault, it was mine. *I* was the one who left Eli alone. *I* was the one who'd been selfish and expected you to be there for me after I hadn't been there for you.'

'It wasn't your fault,' I say automatically.

He smiles. 'I know that now,' he says. 'I didn't always think that way, though. But that's what an accident *is*. No one's to blame. Eli, he — they said he died from shallow-water blackout. He was just swimming, and eventually he'd been holding his breath for too long, and he fainted in the water and he drowned. There are so many variables in a situation like that. Even if we'd been there that day, who's to say it wouldn't have still happened? What if there had been other people in the water? What if it happened half an hour earlier, or half an hour later? If anything about that day had been different, everything might have been fine. But it might not have been either. You can't live in a blame game.'

'But you're mad at me,' I say, grasping for anything that makes sense. 'You said you were mad at me.'

'I was mad that you disappeared right when I needed you,' Cal corrects me. 'I thought you stopped talking to me because Eli's death made you uncomfortable, not because I thought it was your fault.'

'But . . . you didn't talk to me, either,' I say.

We had three years of opportunity. Three years where one of us could've taken the first step, could've sent the first message, could've made the first phone call. But neither of us did.

'I thought you hated me,' Cal says.

'I thought you hated *me*.'

'Well,' Callum says, the smirk propped back up on his face, 'it looks like the root of the problem was a simple lack of communication.'

This time, I smirk along with him.

Because it's not complicated.

It's not complicated at all.

In fact, the problem with our friendship is pretty damn simple.

I reach out and hug him, my arms tight around his neck.

Cal's a great hugger. He's warm and soft and he always smells like fresh baking. He rests his chin against my shoulder and strokes his hand on the back of my head, smoothing out my hair, letting my tears dampen his hoodie.

'You know this isn't the solution to everything,' he says.

'I know.'

'You broke my trust. I'm still not over that.'

'I know.'

'And I'm definitely still mad that you exposed me and Eli at Joe Rooney's party.'

'I know.'

'And, you know, it's not cool of you to scare the shit out of me by walking directly in front of a moving car. That was cruel.' He pulls back to look at me. 'And I know I've been a shitty friend to you, too.'

'It's okay,' I say.

'You need help.' He holds me by the shoulders. 'You *deserve* help.'

I look away, swiping a hand under my nose. 'I know,' I say.

He pulls me back in for a hug.

'But you know I'll be here for you,' he says.

I smile into his chest.

'I know,' I say.

CALLUM

The journey back home is nothing short of complicated.

I make the phone call to Anneke at two a.m. I tell her everything, peppered with a thousand apologies, and she says she'll take an early-morning flight to Wellington. Zelle gets discharged from the hospital at ten the next morning. Anneke meets us there straight from the airport. She looks like hell, but immediately wraps Zelle in a hug.

'I'm sorry,' I tell her, for about the millionth time. To my surprise, she wraps me up in a hug too.

'Thank you for looking after Zelle,' she says. 'You're a good friend.' But when she pulls me back, it's with a hard and serious expression. 'And now you are going to call your mother and explain to her what you've done.'

I wait until we've taken a taxi back to the apartment, where we'll spend the day before the rebooked evening flight to Queenstown. I take my phone to the spare bedroom and sit there for a while before calling. Mum rarely gets furious, but when she does, it's a thing to behold. I'm not ready for the fallout.

'We're going to talk when you get home,' she says, in a voice that turns my insides to jelly. I make a mental note to enjoy these last few hours of freedom, but I'm so exhausted that I crash and spend the rest of the day asleep.

Zelle's doing her best with a departure lounge burger, but looks absolutely drained, wrung out like a bleached sheet from the washing machine. Not to mention the scrapes and grazes across her face and hands.

'I'm so sorry about this, Cal,' Zelle says. She's not the only one relentlessly apologising today.

'You can stop saying that,' I say, trying to be light. 'We both fucked up.'

'Oh my God,' she says. 'The panel. How was it? Shit, I completely forgot.'

I shake my head and look away. 'I didn't go.'

'What? Why not?' I can tell by her tone, though, that she can probably guess the answer.

'I was looking for you.'

'Oh no.' She really does look stricken. 'We went all that way for you and I ruined everything. Again. I'm so sorry, Cal. I'm so sorry.'

I ruffle her blue hair. 'You sound like a broken record.'

'I'm the worst.'

'No, you're not,' I say. '*Never* feel bad for needing help.'

Am I too forgiving? Some people would say yes. Fox

and Mac would. Maybe even Kate. But there's a difference between a flawed person and a bad person, and if the definition of a best friend isn't to be there no matter what, then what would that make me?

And, yeah, I guess I'll have to imagine a future without broadcasting school in it. I have no idea what's next. But do I regret ditching the panel?

Never.

Kate scoops me up in her arms as soon as I'm through the front door. 'Christ, Callum, are you okay?'

'I'm fine,' I say.

'Is Zelle okay?'

I shrug. 'I think so.'.

'Mum's in her room.' She points down the hallway. 'She's *livid*. You better go speak with her.'

Mum's not really the yelling kind, and I'm not the kind who really misbehaves. So, when I see her sitting at her office chair with Descartes purring on her lap, her mouth set in a firm, hard line, I feel a little bit terrified.

'I'm sorry—'

'You don't sneak out and lie about where you are, Callum.' She strokes Descartes' scruffy fur, which causes him to blink his sleepy eyes open. 'Especially not to *Wellington*. I trust you to be a responsible person. You broke my trust this weekend, Cal.'

'I'm really sorry,' I say. 'Look, it's kind of complicated, and I'll explain later, but right now Finn is really mad at me and I need to go see him. Right now. So please delay any groundings or punishments until that's done.'

'You're not going anywhere, mister,' Mum says.

It's a face-off. I sense the people-pleaser, conflict-fearer side of me taking over, begin to feel the hollowness of defeat. But then I hear Zelle's voice in my head, and she says, *Really, Cal? You are SUCH a wet blanket.* And I say, 'Sorry, Mum.'

And I run out of the house.

It takes less than a minute to jog to Finn's front door. I'm out of breath, though, so loiter at the front steps a moment so that I won't sound like I've just escaped a crazy axe-killer. My stomach starts to coil with nerves, but I push down the urge to run back home and crawl under my duvet and never rise again, and pound my fist against the door.

Finn answers. He looks surprised, then annoyed.

I wonder if it's too late to run away.

'You know it's, like, ten o'clock?' he says.

'Sorry.' I look down at my shoes. 'Can I talk to you?'

'I guess.'

'Can I come in?'

'I'm not going to make you stand outside,' he says, opening the door and turning to walk down to his room. I can hear Anwar in the kitchen, but either he doesn't hear us or doesn't want to interrupt. I'm probably enemy number one in the Nassar household.

'How was your weekend?' I say, sitting down in Finn's gaming chair. He's already taken the bed, and I figure it's best to leave some distance. I pick up his Bowser minifigure, stroking my fingers along the creature's smooth plastic skin. 'How was Alex?'

'Not the best,' he says, 'what with my mother trying to guilt-trip me about why I didn't stay with her. And I was beginning to think that maybe she was right.' He glares at me. 'But you didn't come here to talk about my family.'

'I've been a dick,' I burst out, putting down Bowser and picking up Yoshi. 'I'm sorry.'

Finn raises his eyebrows, bemused. 'That's all you've got?'

'I was scared,' I say. I hadn't planned to say this either – God, I don't even *have* a plan – but this feels right. It feels like the truth that's been hiding in a dark corner of my mind, waiting to be found. Saying it out loud is like stretching a muscle that hasn't been used in a long time. Like a release. 'I *am* scared, Finn.'

He looks perplexed. 'Why?'

I don't answer straight away, preparing the words in the mess of my brain. 'Eli was the first relationship I had,' I say. 'Well, the first *everything*. And I was young and naïve and I didn't realise that what was the most significant thing to have ever happened to me was just a bit of messing around for Eli. God, I don't even know if he liked guys. So anyway, he basically ruined my life when he told me the truth, that we were just messing around, that what I thought of our entire summer was just a fantasy in my own head. And we were at the lake together and the rest of the Famous Five were meant to come later, but after Eli told me the news I went on my bike and never came back. And I went and fought with Zelle. And we told Fox and Mac the lake trip was off. And Eli stayed and swam and drowned.'

Finn's silent, but I daren't look at him. I take in a shaky breath and then I continue. 'So like, I kind of hate Eli and what he did to me. But you can't be mad at someone who's dead, right? And, well . . . that day, when I rode away on my bike, I remember thinking I never wanted to see him again. That's how much I hated him. And then it came true and I could never tell anyone that's how I felt, because how much of a horrible person would that make me?'

'You're not a horrible person —' Finn starts, but I keep going.

'So anyway, after that day, I've been scared. I like you. But every time we're together, I think about everything that could go wrong. All the ways we could be ruined. Because something will ruin us. One day. Probably.'

I don't notice the tears stinging my eyes until Finn leans forward and clasps my hands in his. He smiles. 'It's very offensive how little faith you have in me, Callum,' he says.

I laugh, but it sounds like a choke. 'I think I care about you too much to risk getting hurt by you,' I whisper.

Finn places his hand on my jaw. Tentatively. Like a question.

I let him. I lean into him.

'Life is a *bitch*, Callum,' he says. 'But you can't spend your whole life trying to run from hurt at the expense of experiencing something that could actually be great. And, in my humble opinion, I think you and me would be pretty great.'

'School finishes in, like, two months,' I say.

'Thank God for that.'

'We might be moving to different cities next year.'

'That's a problem for next year.'

'I'm scared.'

'You're overthinking this, Callum.'

'I can't help it.'

And then he leans forward and kisses me.

His lips taste sweet, like he ate something sugary before. He starts slow, cautious, like he's asking another question.

In answer I open my lips wider. Drape my hand on the back of his neck and run my fingers through his hair. This time, I kiss him back properly.

This time, I don't pull away.

Finn moves his head and presses his cheek against mine — hard. His nose nudges my cheekbone.

'Worth the risk?' he asks.

I kiss the crown of his head. 'I think so.'

ZELLE

When we finally make it back to The Sanctuary, Mum bursts into tears.

I haven't seen her cry so hard since the day Dad announced he was leaving. Even with all the shit I've done in the past three years, she's rarely gotten upset, just yelled and slammed doors and locked herself in her room to paint. It feels like I'm looking at some strange, alien specimen cosplaying as my mother.

I don't know what to say.

Mum wraps her arms around me. 'I'm so glad you're okay, Zella.'

I burrow my face into the fabric of her blouse until I can feel the soft thrum of her heartbeat against my ear.

'You're not mad?' I say.

'Of course I'm mad, *koekert*. But mostly I'm just worried.'

I'm crying now, too, and for a moment we just stay like

that, breathing heavily, choking on our tears.

I can't remember the last time I hugged my mum like this.

When I was a kid, probably.

Far too long ago.

'I'm so sorry,' I sob. And, because it doesn't feel like enough, I say it in Dutch: '*Het spijt me, mama.*'

Mum pulls away to look down at me, and there's an expression in her eyes that is so foreign, I barely recognise it for what it is: compassion. Love, even. 'It's okay, Gisella,' she says.

And that makes me cry even more.

'Shh,' Mum says, rubbing my back, drawing small circles up and down my spine like she used to do when I was young. 'Talk to me.'

And we do. We talk. For hours.

Mum asks me to recount everything that happened in Wellington, which turns into a talk about Callum, which turns into a talk about Dad, and Eli, and that last summer.

I tell her everything that happened between me and Cal, right up to the day Eli died and after. How I felt like I couldn't face him again. How I felt like I didn't deserve to face him again.

Mum listens the whole way through and doesn't interrupt, not even when the clock ticks past midnight. She lets me talk, and when I've finished, I collapse against her, and it's the first time in years that I've let her put her arm around me like this.

'I wish I'd known this before,' she says softly, playing with my hair.

I shrug. I'm all cried out, but that doesn't stop fresh tears from pricking my eyes. 'I stopped feeling close to you,' I say.

Mum's lips are pressed into a tight line. 'I love you,' she says.

'I love you, too.'

'Things need to change,' Mum says, with enough firmness to be a comfort: like the mum I know. 'You're going to stop drinking. And you're going to keep seeing that counsellor every week. Understood?'

I pull away, drawing my knees up to my chest. 'Understood.'

'I want you to be well, Zella.' She pushes her hair off her shoulders. I hadn't noticed until now how much it's grown since we left Wellington; it falls further down her back now, making her look younger. 'I'll do whatever it takes to get you better.'

It's too much to meet her eye. I look down at the tattered couch, pulling a loose thread out from the seam.

'Thank you,' I say.

She keeps her fingers in my hair.

'Let's get some sleep,' she says.

CALLUM

I'm surfing the internet on my laptop when the email comes through.

It's from broadcasting school. I already know it'll be a rejection, so I open it without thinking.

Dear Callum,

We are pleased to inform you that your application into the Bachelor of Communication (Journalism Studies) programme has been successful.

This must be a mistake.

I read it again.

And again.

How?

I fire off a text to Zelle.

got an email from broadcasting school saying I got in?!?! genuinely think this must be a mistake

definitely not a mistake, Zelle replies almost instantly.

glad to see my plan worked

What?

what???? I say.

I figured I owed you after that train wreck of a trip to wellington, Zelle types. *I emailed that girl — jazz? — and explained that it was my fault u couldn't go on the panel. then I emailed the head of admissions and told them your missed interview was on me as well. they said I couldn't directly influence their decision — rude, am I right? — but that they'd take those circumstances into consideration*

OH MY GOD, I write. *THANK YOU*

it's all you, cal. u got in on your own merit

YOU'RE THE BEST

well, duh

THANK YOU THANK YOU THANK YOU

That's what best friends are for :)

Councillor Steps Down from Local Body Elections

Keri Elliot, Editor-in-Chief, Stakesville Chronicle

Councillor for the Stakesville ward in the Central Otago Regional Council, Tim Cooney, has pulled out of his candidacy in the upcoming local body elections. In a statement released by his office late yesterday, Cooney announced he was stepping down to focus on his family and business.

'It is with a heavy heart that I have decided to pull out of the running in this year's local government elections, scheduled to take place on October 14,' Cooney said. 'This decision was not made lightly, and I will continue to serve my community in my role as a husband, father and business owner.'

Cooney recently made headlines after an interview published in error by the *Stakesville Chronicle* accused Cooney of making disparaging remarks about the LGBTQIA+ community. The article was removed and the reporter, Callum Rig, was stood down with immediate effect. Cooney's statement emphasised that this was not the reason he was pulling out of his candidacy.

'My stepping down has nothing to do with the recent controversy surrounding the interview published by Callum Rig,' his statement said. 'This is an issue I have paid deep consideration to for a long time. Recently, personal circumstances have reinforced my decision that it is time for me to hand the reins to someone else.'

Tim Cooney has served on the Central Otago Regional Council for one term. Co-owner of Perfect Mistakes café, Martin Villiers, last week announced his candidacy in the election.

EPILOGUE
CALLUM

'Are you sure about this?'

Talking Heads is blasting through the car as we drive along the highway from Mistakesville to the lake. Finn is shotgun — boyfriend privileges. Zelle, Fox and Mac are crammed in the back. Currently, they're talking about Tim Cooney's decision not to run in the election. I allow my eyes to dart briefly to Finn's before focusing back on the road.

'You don't have to come,' I say. 'Not if you don't want to.'

'No, I want to,' Finn says quickly. 'I'm just worried that maybe I shouldn't be here. I mean, I never met Eli.'

'Well, you're meeting him now.'

At the turnoff to the unsealed road that cuts through the sloping hill and down to the lake, I slow down and squeeze Finn's knee. 'He'd want you to come,' I say quietly, and I can tell he's smiling at me.

As we get closer, all of us go quiet. My chest aches already, remembering the last time I was down this road, hurtling on my bike, tears streaming. Zelle catches my eye in the rear-view mirror and smiles, but I can see she's nervous, too.

Things aren't perfect between us. While Mac and Fox have been open-minded, they're still frosty with Zelle, and we're still far from being the Famous Five we once were – or if we can ever be. But we're spending time together, and Zelle hasn't drunk since that night in Wellington, and it feels like we're building back the trust we once had. And it turns out that's not such a complicated task after all.

We pull up at the carpark above the lake. When the engine's off and the music dies, no one moves. It's a sunny, bright day, still too cold for swimming, but there are a few other cars parked up and some people down on the shoreline. Eli's death made the papers, but when they reported that his drowning wasn't circumstantial – that he was a strong swimmer in a safe lake, simply afflicted by the little-known consequences of holding your breath too long – daytrippers soon returned. People are quick to forget.

'I can't believe we've never been here,' Mac says.

At once three years feels like the longest time and also like no time at all. I close my eyes for a moment and imagine Eli, his face and his voice and his laugh so easy to conjure up as if I had only seen him yesterday. But trying to imagine him also feels impossible, because so much has changed. Because *I've* changed. What would he be like now?

'Callum?' Finn says, tapping my shoulder. 'Are you all right?'

I open my eyes and nod. 'Should we go?' I say.

And we do.

We're silent as we make our way from the car down to the lakeside. Around a bend on the shore, at a rocky outcrop a few hundred metres away from the main jetty, is where a memorial was set up for Eli. It's the same spot where his body was found. I don't know who maintains it – the Gibson family haven't been back since they moved, and Eli has his own grave in a family plot at a cemetery in Canterbury. I'm gripped by a sudden worry. What if there isn't anything there now?

We turn a corner and, right there on the rock, is a bouquet of artificial flowers and Eli's name engraved in the stone. My breath catches in my throat and I stand there, frozen. Finn leans his shoulder against me, and on my left side a hand grabs mine. I turn around. It's Zelle.

Her eyes are misty and guilt darkens her features. Fox and Mac look just as tearful. Wordlessly, we huddle together, Zelle and Finn flanking me either side, Fox and Mac leaning their heads on my shoulders.

We're not the same Famous Five we once were, and we never will be. But I like where we are now. And I think we'll be okay.

ACKNOWLEDGEMENTS

Thank you to…

My family and friends (that includes you, flatmates!).

The whole team at Allen & Unwin, for taking a chance on me.

Jane Parkin, whose deft edits have made this story so much better.

Christa Moffitt, for the fantastic cover design.

Kate Duignan and the rest of the MA crew, for keeping me sane during a hectic year.

The New Zealand Society of Authors, Creative New Zealand, and the Storylines Charitable Trust, for providing the funding, opportunities and awards that have got this novel where it is.

Karen Trebilcock, for being my first writing mentor.

Mandy Hager, who read and assessed an earlier draft of this novel.

Ebony Lamb, for the beautiful author photo.

And finally, to my real-life Callum, who makes me both a better writer and a better person.

© Ebony Lamb

ABOUT THE AUTHOR

Hannah Marshall has an MA in Creative Writing from the International Institute of Modern Letters at Te Herenga Waka—Victoria University of Wellington. She's been a winner of the Maurice Gee Prize in Children's Writing, an NZSA CompleteMS Manuscript Assessment recipient and she won the Best Unpublished Author category in the Storylines Tessa Duder YA Award 2024.

This is her first novel.